THE KEY OF GOLD

by

Jan Hathaway

Author of "Junior Nurse" *and*
"Treasure of the Redwoods"

In each life there is a moment in time when April becomes May; when toys are put away forever; when reality
becomes almost as interesting as dreams and awareness of
responsibility to self and to society takes possession of the
mind. For Evalin Mitchell, the moment came when she
was sixteen and went as usual to spend the summer in
Princess Town, Maryland, with her grandmother.

She found the ruggedly independent old lady on
crutches and unable to operate the little ferryboat service
to Carter's Hollow which was her livelihood. Since there
was no money to pay an operator, the obvious solution
to the problem was for Evalin to take over. Yet this
meant giving up the recreation and fun the girl had
planned.

THE KEY OF GOLD

THE KEY OF GOLD

by

JAN HATHAWAY

Alouette Romance
By
Sharon Publications, Inc.
Closter, NJ

THE KEY OF GOLD

Chapter 1

Just beyond the crab cannery lay a broad marshland that appeared to be a favorite haunt of ducks and sea gulls and bitterns. Evalin Mitchell estimated that at least a thousand birds had gathered there, noisy creatures all and some less friendly than they ought to be. Near a big, moss-splotched rock, two gulls were actually having a battle of nerves. The smaller was guarding a fish or some other type of food that flashed silver in the hot June sunshine. The larger gull kept charging in for the food, feinting with its beak, fanning its wings, now squawking, now snapping. The larger gull's idea seemed to be to frighten the smaller gull away, for no bodily contact was ever made, nor was a feather even tweaked. Naturally, Evalin rooted for the smaller gull to stand its ground. Had she been close enough, she might have done something to help it. Then the smaller gull charged. Taken by surprise, the larger gull had to do some fancy stepping to avoid being nipped. Now both birds squawked and fanned their wings, but the larger definitely retreated. Evalin cheered. "Right triumphs over might!" she predicted to Mr. Pike. "Behold!"

But a disgusting thing happened.

As casually as you please, a third gull swooped low and made off with the silvery food. At once the battle ended. An exciting chase began. Fully two hundred other gulls joined the chase, and for a time all the powder blue sky seemed filled with pumping wings and screeching, wide-open mouths. But there was no justice in the bird world, it developed. Down the throat of the thief went the food. It gave one gulp, one unashamed swish of its tail, and the incident was over. Presently all the birds were back in the marshland, some cooling off in the greenish puddles, others dozing on one leg in the shade.

Mr. Pike said philosophically: "Well, that happens. And you can't even say it's unfair, really, because Nature has her own code: survival of the fittest! That's the first law of Nature, you know."

"Then it's time someone repealed the law. The idea!"

Mr. Pike looked at his pocket watch. "Too bad it's so late. I wanted to show you some ferns. You can see more impressive ferns in a rain forest, of course, but you won't see bigger ones anywhere here in Maryland."

Evalin was puzzled. She wondered why Mr. Pike had arranged for someone to pick her up in the marshland and drive her to Dr. McGrath's office in Birch Corners. What in the world could she do for her grandmother or anyone else in Dr. McGrath's office? Furthermore, her grandmother would rage. Her grandmother had never liked spies and never would.

As if he had sensed her puzzlement, Mr. Pike said gruffly: "Humor me, Evalin, please. The truth is, I think Mrs. Murdock is keeping things from me. You know how she is."

Evalin tucked her back shirt tail down into her denim slacks. She wished she had been told in advance that someone would be driving her to Birch Corners. All the girls in Birch Corners were elegant dressers. Compared with them, she would look sloppy. And suppose one of her Princess Town admirers had a chance to see her in Birch Corners on the same street with an elegant dresser? The end of her magical summer! Right then and there would be ended every hope of giving the Princess Town boys a bad time!

Rumbling sounds interrupted Evalin's thoughts. Every bird fell silent, every beak swung east. The sounds grew identifiable at last as those made by a truck coming along the eastern edge of the marshland via the oyster-shell road. Oddly enough, the moment the pickup truck came into sight, many of the ducks and all the bitterns nipped off to hide in the tall grass and weeds. Not the gulls, however! Either braver or more sophisticated than the other birds, the gulls went on with their affairs quite as if they had the marshland to themselves.

Mr. Pike said quickly, almost beggingly, "I'm not asking you to betray your grandmother, you understand. But if she has to take things easier, I want to know. I have to know, don't I? How can I look after her if I don't know what's going on?"

"I've told you, Mr. Pike."

"No."

Evalin started to cross her heart. She stopped, remembering that was a juvenile habit she had vowed to break that summer. "If you won't believe me," she asked, "what can I say? Grammy was supposed to take some pills to improve her blood circulation. Grammy was careless. So a blood vessel ruptured in her legs and she has to be on crutches. That's everything I know."

"What about her heart?"

"Well, it could be better, according to Dr. Mc-Grath, but she isn't going to die or have a stroke or anything."

"How do you know that?"

The truck driver was Ted Pillsbury. The moment she recognized him, Evalin felt betrayed. "Really!" she sputtered. "Of all the boys in town!"

"If Mrs. Murdock needs help, he's strong enough."

Evalin gave Mr. Pike that big, brown-eyed, reproachful stare that had served her so well at Cantwell High throughout her sophomore year. If he noticed, he gave no sign. "Things have to change around here," Mr. Pike said firmly. "Now that Mrs. Murdock and I are practically engaged, I'll have to take over more. You tell her that. You tell her Sam Pike is taking over."

Ted Pillsbury eased the truck to a smooth halt about ten feet behind them. He was gallant for a change. He neither beeped nor sat in the truck cab like a Roman Emperor waiting for a mortified girl to come to him. Not only did he escort Evalin to the truck, but he helped her up to the front seat as well. And he actually drove like a sensible person, never exceeding twenty miles an hour until they had reached the end of the oyster-shell road. Then, on the highway to Birch Corners, Ted speeded up to thirty-five miles an hour and held that pace steadily.

"You should've telephoned," Ted said. "I'd have come for you. Why didn't you call?"

He was a strange boy, Evalin decided. Just yesterday afternoon in Margie's Hut, who had ordered her to fade from his life? Mr. Ted Pillsbury!

"City kids are confusing," Ted went on. "They never seem to learn that in the country everybody helps each other. Why's that?"

"People are people the world over."

"Yeah?"

"Yes."

"How do you know?"

The question annoyed Evalin. What a wonderful thing it would be if just for a while, just for a day or so, people would stop asking her how she knew this and how she knew that. It was such a silly question! How did anyone know anything? How did a person know, for instance, that the sun rose and set every day of the year, visibly or invisibly? You just knew, period.

"Anyhow," Ted said, "I'm glad Mr. Pike telephoned. I'm sort of sorry about yesterday afternoon."

"Are you, now! I was never so insulted in my life!"

"Things get mixed up sometimes, Evalin. Don't you ever get mixed up?"

The confession, then the pleading question, rather bothered Evalin. She stole a shy glance at his face, not knowing whether he was speaking sincerely or cold-bloodedly aiming his words at a girl's emotions. If things were really mixed up for him, then she could forgive him. She certainly understood what it was like to be mixed up about things. All this last year she had been mixed up most of the time. Take her studying, for example. During her freshman year she had known the value of studying and she had studied faithfully five evenings a week even when studying bored her. She had gotten straight A's. But this year, even though she had still known the value of studying, she had been unable to settle down with her books evening after evening. So many different emotions had pulled her in so many different directions! One moment she was studying, the next moment she was chattering on the telephone, the next moment she was playing her dance records, and the next moment she was rushing outdoors for a breath of fresh air or to join the gang in a quick soda.

"Ah, don't sulk," Ted said. "For your information, everybody thinks you're the nicest summer girl who comes to Princess Town. You want to ruin your reputation?"

It excited Evalin. "Really, Ted? Is that what they say?"

"One thing I never do is lie."

The truck crested a little hill. Birch Corners could be seen about five miles away, a quite pretty, pink-roofed town partially screened on all sides by lovely stands of birch trees. Evalin loved the sight, and suddenly she loved being with handsome, brawny, golden-haired, blue-eyed Ted Pillsbury in the cab of his father's truck.

"To answer your original question," she told him, "I often get mixed up. But I don't worry about it, and do you know why? Because according to Mom, mental and emotional confusion go hand in hand with being an adolescent. I can't clue you in on everything, because it's a pretty complicated subject. But what it boils down to, according to Mom, is that we're confused because we haven't yet found our places in the world. So you know what I do? I just go along from day to day and refuse to be panicked by confusion."

Ted mulled that over, his forehead crinkled charmingly.

"Of course," Evalin admitted, "I do panic sometimes. I just can't seem to help it. But when that happens I say to myself: Gleek! Then everything is all right again."

"Gleek? What does that do?"

"Stops the panic. Don't ask me why. Dad told me it works, and it does."

They reached Dr. McGrath's brick medical building on Nainsworth Drive. As luck would have it, three girls came along, each an elegant dresser, each with her hair just so. Self-conscious about her tired blouse and old denim slacks, Evalin lost no time getting into the medical building before the girls got close enough for Ted to make some shattering comparisons. Not that she was going to become involved steadily with any one particular boy this summer, but the less—

Evalin never finished the thought. Sitting sort of scrooched together in an armchair near the reception-room window, her grandmother said, "Girl, take me home, please."

There was a quality in her voice that made Evalin feel bitter cold.

Grammy said: "I'll never come here again. Girl, do you hear? I'll never come here again."

Dr. McGrath came in, tall and thin, his wrinkled face looking weary. Grammy said: "You won't beach me, sawbones, if I have to pin your ears to my ferryboat." She said it twice. Each time, Dr. McGrath muttered, "There, there, now, easy does it."

He gestured for Evalin to join him in his office. Like her father's office in faraway Cantwell, Massachusetts, the room was small and cluttered and pungent with the smell of antiseptics. Three cabinets of instruments and other equipment ran the length of one wall. Under the single window was a crowded bookcase. Evalin spotted *Gray's Anatomy* and *Dorland's Illustrated Medical Dictionary* while she was waiting for Dr. McGrath to sit down.

Dr. McGrath asked suddenly: "Can you take it, Evalin? According to Mrs. Murdock, you're the only relative she has in the States just now."

His expression almost panicked Evalin. All too often, in the past, she had seen the same "bad news" expression on her father's face. Under her breath she said fiercely: "Gleek!" Panic stopped, but not the cold sensation in her hands and legs.

"The fact is," Dr. McGrath announced, "that Mrs. Murdock needs supervision. She's been told to do as little walking as possible, but she's been running her ferryboat, leg or no leg, coronary problems notwithstanding. Well, what do I do? I know that Dr. and Mrs. Mitchell are doing important work in Thailand this summer. On the other hand, I have a duty to Mrs. Murdock, my patient."

Evalin swallowed hard.

"Now actually," Dr. McGrath went on, "I think that rest and medication will get your grandmother off crutches in two months. If she's reasonably intelligent and develops no other physical malfunctions, she ought to live to sass me for a good many years. She's only sixty or so, after all. But she must have rest and she must take her medicine. Understood?"

Tears came. Evalin tried to hold them back, but they came anyway.

Dr. McGrath asked sternly, "What does crying solve? Stop being a baby! This is a problem, nothing more. You attack problems with your mind, not tears. You of all people ought to know that! You're a surgeon's daughter, you're a nurse's daughter."

He pointed at a box of Kleenex, and Evalin took two sheets and dabbed embarrassedly at her moist eyes.

"My orders are these," Dr. McGrath said. "Your grandmother is to stay off her feet for two months. Oh, she can walk from one chair to another, things like that. But she isn't to cheat any more as she's been cheating far too long. Definitely, she is not to work on her boat. She can sit there, yes, or even steer if she remains seated, but she is not to behave like a roustabout any longer. Is that clear?"

"Yes, sir."

Dr. McGrath nodded. Quite as if his words had not just smashed Grammy's life into smithereens, he went grinningly to Grammy to help her into the pickup truck.

Chapter 2

Evalin cooked a light dinner for three in the small, red-curtained galley of the *Sea Hawk*. From time to time she listened for temper "squalls," determined to intervene if her grandmother became too excited. But there was little conversation on the aft starboard deck, and what little there was happened to be quite pleasant. It suddenly occurred to Evalin that in his quiet, jolly way Mr. Pike was a great man. For almost a full hour after Ted had returned them to Murdock House, Grammy had sat frozen-faced and scared on the deep front porch. Nothing Evalin had said had appeared to reach her. Evalin had finally become so worried she had given serious thought to telephoning Dr. McGrath. At that moment Mr. Pike had come ambling along, his roundish face pink and clean, every wisp of his gray hair in place, his blue duck trousers starched and pressed, his yellow sweat shirt turned up just so about his large middle. A wave of his hand, a smile, a comment about the river spread before them, and the next thing Evalin knew, Grammy's face had become normal again and she had begun to chatter as if never in her life would there be enough time for her to say all she wanted to say. Every once in a while, of course, there had been temper "squalls." One had been quite fierce. Grammy had suggested they eat aboard the ferryboat. Mr. Pike had grinned and said, "Well, if you're silly enough to let me carry you, Mrs. Murdock, I'm silly enough to try."

"Carry me? Preposterous! Why should I be carried? How dare you say I'm a helpless old cripple!"

"Orders are orders. Now be a good girl and get up so I can grab you. Whether you like it or not, Sam Pike is taking over."

Grammy had sputtered throughout the hun-

dred-foot journey to the *Sea Hawk*. But never once
had Mr. Pike lost patience with her; indeed, he
had chuckled or grinned all the time he was carrying her, pretending the whole thing was a lark.
So at last Grammy had gotten aboard her beloved
boat, and her temper had certainly improved.

Working in the galley, Evalin decided to have
a long chat with Mr. Pike about the technique he
had used so successfully with Grammy. Exactly
what had he done there on the porch to snap
Grammy out of her doldrums? And exactly what
was he doing there on the deck to slow Grammy
down to a pleasant conversational crawl. It
seemed to Evalin that she had to learn to use that
technique, and in a hurry, if she were going to do
some good around there. Another thing: what
was she to do about money and such? According
to her parents, Grammy had not had much money
since Gramps had died. The income from Grammy's ferryboat service to Carter Hollow had provided her a simple living through her widowhood
years, but that was all. Well, then, how could
food bills and other expenses be paid if the ferry-

boat were kept tied up all summer while Grammy was following Dr. McGrath's orders?

A quail call interrupted Evalin's thoughts. Pleasantly surprised, Evalin stuck her head out the starboard porthole and quail-called back to Mary-Ann Bishop. A fetching sight in white shorts and blouse, MaryAnn skimmed her red canoe quite close to the *Sea Hawk* and called in her merry way: "A line, a line, I beseech a line!" As Evalin loped happily to the deck to throw her a line, Grammy called: "Where's chow? I'm starving, Mouse! Do you want me to starve?"

Evalin generously gave the adults on deck the whole mushroom omelette she had prepared. With the omelette she served sliced tomatoes and peas, toasted rolls and gooseberry jam and coffee. When she returned to the galley she found Mary-Ann breaking six eggs into the frying pan. Mary-Ann said crisply: "Sit and give. My, the tales you hear in town! How on earth did you talk Ted Pillsbury into giving you a lift?"

"Mr. Pike arranged that. Do you know something about Ted? Ted can be the kindest, most

considerate boy in Princess Town. The moment
we got Grammy into the truck Ted knew she was
all upset. So to make her laugh he told her the
funniest story about a turtle that thought it was a
chicken. Grammy did laugh, too."

"Sue Winthrop was furious."

"I shudder."

"She really told Ted off, too. Right in front of
everyone in the Strawberry Goo, she gave him a
real Winthrop frying. So on Yacht Club Day she's
dating Mike Tilburn."

"Not if Ted wants to date her," Evalin dis-
agreed. "Smooth, smooth, smooth."

MaryAnn's black eyes asked a question.

A bit embarrassed, Evalin almost refused to answer it. Still, Evalin thought, what was the point
of having practically a sister if you kept everything about yourself a dark secret?

"Candidly," she told MaryAnn, "I'm on probation this summer. Something happened to me last
year back home. I wasn't wild, exactly, but I certainly wasn't a model teen-ager. For some reason,
everything seemed so dull, such a dreadful bore."

MaryAnn said excitedly: "My!" She flipped the fried eggs onto plates and got a carton of milk from the little icebox. "You talk and I'll eat," MaryAnn said. "The confessions of a bored teenager! How exciting!"

Evalin talked, having started, but she made certain she got her share of the eggs, bread, jam, and milk.

"Well," she went on, "my marks were a disgrace, and I was certainly the maverick of the sophomore class. Finally my parents put their feet down. It was coming to me, I suppose. Anyway, no car of my own unless Grammy gives them a good report at the end of the summer."

Exasperatingly, MaryAnn proved she had a one-track mind. "No dates, in other words?"

"Not until I prove I'm worthy of them, to practically quote Mom. According to Mom, I'm pretty cold-blooded and cruel. She said I ought to be ashamed of myself for using my beauty to give boys a bad time. I suppose I did, really. But they're so darned silly! They ask for it! Why, there was one boy who actually wanted me to be his steady!

That's crazy!"

MaryAnn nodded. "I ran into the same thing last year, too," MaryAnn said. "The first thing I knew, this particular boy was waylaying me in the halls at school. Wherever I went, there he was, smiling and waiting. Well, I finally went to a football game with him. That did it for fair! Every time I went out with another boy that month, he had a fight with the boy. So you know what I did? I went out with a nice senior I know, and this time there wasn't any fight, you can bet on that. And then I told this boy he was silly and I laughed at him in front of everyone. Now he hates me. I don't think he'd go out with me if I actually paid him to."

Mr. Pike came into the galley. He grinned. "Looks like a serious conference," he commented. "I hope you're both being kind to Ted. Ted's all right."

MaryAnn said: "Three cheers for Ted!" She jumped up and waved her arms energetically and yelled: "Rah, rah, rah!"

Mr. Pike suggested she go on deck and clown

around to amuse Mrs. Murdock. MaryAnn got the message and zipped out of the galley. Whatever she did when she reached Grammy must have been quite amusing, for suddenly Grammy really did laugh.

Evalin said wistfully: "I wish I could be that way, Mr. Pike. Everything is fun for MaryAnn, so she makes fun for everybody. But she's no dim-witted clown, either. I actually think MaryAnn would be an honor student even if she never opened a book."

"Nonsense. Knowledge has to be acquired, and you don't acquire it without effort. May I ask a frank question?"

"I guess so."

"How's the money situation around here?"

Evalin drew a deep breath. Kid stuff or not, at times like this she wished her mother were around to give a girl advice.

"Now you listen to me," Mr. Pike said sternly, "and listen closely. One of these days, Mrs. Murdock and I will be married. You may not think so and she may not think so, but it will happen. So

I have the right to ask a question as personal as that. Believe me, I wouldn't ask it if I doubted I had the right."

"But—"

"Can she get by and pay her bills if this boat is tied up all summer?"

Evalin decided she could answer the question honestly, so she did. "I really don't know," she answered. "My folks seem to think Grammy just makes a bare living with the boat. I know that Dad sends her a check every month, and Grammy returns the check, and then Dad always yells: 'But she can't be making more than a bare living with that boat!' Then Dad always reminds Mom that Grammy is *her* mother, and he tells Mom to lay the law down to Grammy. Mom always writes a letter, and Grammy ignores it, and by that time another month has rolled around and the whole thing is repeated."

Mr. Pike gave a mock shudder that made Evalin smile. Loyally, Evalin said, "Not that Grammy has foolish pride, you understand. It's just that she wants to live here and run the ferryboat and be independent."

"In that case, she certainly won't accept money from me. All right. Then we'll consider the second idea I had. According to Dr. McGrath, she can supervise the operation of the boat and even steer it if she stays off her feet. Well, suppose she hired a young fellow to do all the running and the heavy work?"

Evalin shook her head, having already considered that idea herself. "Grammy once told me," she said, "that business is good enough to support just one person, not two."

He considered that information, his eyes never leaving Evalin's thin, lightly freckled face. After a time he finally asked the question Evalin had feared he would ask. Just like that he asked, "Well, what about you helping her operate the boat? I could look after the engine and such and even relieve you on weekends. You'd earn your keep, and you'd certainly be doing something you could be proud of all your life."

But the trouble with that, Evalin thought, was that her summer vacation would be ruined. She certainly had not come to the Eastern Shore of Maryland to work. She had come to sail, to play tennis, to explore the great outdoors. Yes, and she had come to zoom around town with girls and fellows her own age. All that was what summer had been made for! You were only young once! There were only just so many carefree summers a person could have. Next year, for example, she would go with her father and mother to Thailand, perhaps to work with kids her own age in a village near the Chiengmai River. Then college; then work every summer thereafter! Why, this was really the last summer of her youth!

"You can do it," Mr. Pike said flatly. "You have Murdock blood in you, too, so you can do it and you will do it."

For a moment Evalin resented his tone of voice.

Mr. Pike asked softly, "Or don't you love her at all, Evalin?"

He rose and left before Evalin could answer.

Chapter 3

It was a predicament strange to Evalin Mitchell. Not before in her sixteen years and five weeks of life had she been faced with the necessity of making an unaided decision on so serious a matter as that involving her grandmother's well-being. The necessity frightened her. She knew enough about her own temperament and character to doubt her ability either to make wise decisions or to abide by them once they had been made. All her life, for instance, she had hated doing the same thing day after day after day. Well, the work on the ferryboat would certainly be a day-after-day-after-day thing. Ten trips a day to Carter Hollow; ten trips a day back to Princess Town. First trip out at six in the morning; last trip back at eight in the evening. And every trip would have to be begun on time and ended on time, and always the same course would have to be sailed, because fuel was expensive and any impulsive wanderings would be costly. How about that! Within a week the sameness of the work and the monotony of the schedule would drive her stark, staring mad! Yet if she decided to help her grandmother operate the boat, she would have to abide by that decision, crazy or not!

Then what about her ability to cope with Grammy the Independent, Grammy the Crafty, Grammy the Warm-hearted and Charming? Suppose out there on the water some day Grammy decided to stand up behind the brass-handled steering wheel? Or suppose Grammy decided that "just a little walk" would do no harm? It would certainly be difficult, if not impossible, for an inexperienced teen-ager to make Grammy follow Dr. McGrath's orders exactly. Grammy might jump to her feet just to prove she was still the captain of her own life. Or Grammy might convince her with crafty talk that "this once" a walk would be all right. Or Grammy might so charm her with those twinkling eyes and that gay Murdock smile it would be impossible for a girl not to humor her.

Evalin thought gloomily that she ought to have insisted upon going to faraway Thailand with her parents. There might have been problems in Thailand, too, but at least her parents would have been available to give her guidance in the solution of those problems. Darn it, how did *they* go about meeting the challenges of the problems they ran into in those Asiatic villages where they had worked every summer for the past nine years? Of course, the first thing they did was identify the problem, for how could you meet a problem's challenge until you knew what those challenges really were?

Then something seemed to click in Evalin's mind.

She swallowed hard. For a moment she felt so ashamed of herself she had a silly urge to punish herself with a good pinching. Why was she brooding there when the solution to one of Grammy's problems, the problem of how Grammy was to get around, was so perfectly obvious?

Evalin went back to her bedroom on the second floor of Murdock House and changed her clothes from the skin out. Remembering that Mrs. Winthrop had always liked her in pink and that Mrs. Winthrop preferred skirts to shorts or slacks, Evalin got out the pink icing coordinates her parents' housekeeper had bought through a Sears Roebuck mail-order catalogue as a going-away present for her. It was just the sort of thing Molly *would* buy, Evalin decided, looking at her reflection in the mirror. To Molly, doggone it, she would always be a "doll baby" to dress up in candy stripes and lace! There was lace, all right: lace-flounced sleeves, lace-banded skirt! Yet to be fair to Molly as well as to Sears Roebuck, it was a darned cute, even perky ensemble. White shoes, of course, rather than sandals, to give herself the height the full skirt needed. White gloves, too, if she was to prove to Mrs. Winthrop that she showed promise of becoming a lady!

On the porch, Grammy said, "Sweet." Sarcasm gave the word bite. "Oh, you've Murdock blood in you," Grammy went on. "Your mother was always working that trick when she wanted something. All prettied up, sweet enough to kiss, but her mind conniving every second of the time."

"Really?"

"Girl, if you've prettied up for a date, get yourself unprettied. I know all about you; don't think I don't! The night before you came, your mother talked to me over the telephone for a good ten minutes. Well, I've got the cure for that sort of high jinks. Work. Look at the *Sea Hawk!* You get your working pants on and give her a good swabbing down!"

"Actually," Evalin told her, "this is a sort of social visit. I thought I'd talk to Mrs. Winthrop a few minutes."

"And what does a Murdock have to do with society ladies like Mrs. Winthrop?"

"It so happens, Grammy, that Mrs. Winthrop is a very nice lady. Anyway, Dad told me to be sure to call on her. Mrs. Winthrop gives the medical school Dad teaches in about ten thousand dollars every year. Also, she finds jobs for patients after they've been discharged from the university's hospital."

"I don't like her."

Adults, Evalin thought, could sometimes be downright confusing. Take Grammy right now. Grammy always gave her a real Murdock frying whenever she said she definitely disliked this or that person. If if was wrong for a girl to dislike a person, why was it right for Grammy to dislike Mrs. Winthrop?

Grammy looked irritably at her gold baguette wristwatch. "Well, you can take an hour," Grammy finally said. "Not a minute more, though. We have to powwow about a lot of things. Also, you'll swab the *Sea Hawk* today or I'll know the reason why. It so happens I like a shipshape boat."

Relieved, Evalin saluted, said, "Aye, aye, ma'am," and hurried on. But as it turned out, Evalin never did see Mrs. Winthrop that morning. When she reached the grounds of the lovely Winthrop estate at the foot of the Strand, Evalin found

Sue Winthrop and Ted Pillsbury playing a game of miniature golf on the front lawn. Ted grinned and waved, and Sue was incredibly cordial. Sue called: "My favorite candy-striped doll! Hi, Evalin, what a nice surprise!"

Sue bent over her golf ball, her feet close together, her blonde hair stirring in a river breeze. Sue's objective was to drive the golf ball up a little red ramp and through the O-shaped mouth of a gaudily painted clown. If the ball just grazed the inner left-hand side of the clown's mouth, it would carom off to the right and head straight for the Number 12 hole. With luck, Sue would score a hole-in-one.

Ted joshed: "You'll never do it, Sue. It takes strong nerves and lots of skill to play this hole in four shots."

"Hush!"

Ted hushed.

Sue brought her stick down smartly and the ball zipped up the red ramp. The ball did graze the inner left-hand side of the clown's mouth, but Sue had hit it so forcefully the ball caromed too sharply. It angled off to the right of the Number 12 hole and ended up in the water trap.

Sue rolled her pretty green eyes. "Some days are like that," she lamented.

As Evalin headed for the magnificent white frame house, however, Sue flipped her club to Ted and joined Evalin on the walkway. "Mother's out," Sue announced, "and Pop's north on business. How's Mrs. Murdock?"

"Fine."

Sue gave her a peculiar glance that told Evalin the news had gotten around town.

"Well," Evalin amended, "that's what I told Grammy this morning. She was pretty blue, so I had to say something to cheer her up."

"Personally," Sue confided, "I hate to be around sick people. They're always so gloomy and whiny they end up by making me feel gloomy, too. Are you sending for your folks?"

"I haven't decided. Actually, I'm sort of confused right now. Dr. McGrath seems to think Grammy will do just fine if she takes things easy. But I'm not sure I can make her behave. Even

Mom has trouble making Grammy behave."

"Well, I'd handle that in exactly one minute," Sue announced. "I'd lay down the law. Behave, or else."

"Or else what?"

"Or else I'd leave her flat."

"But suppose she still didn't behave, what then?"

"I'd leave her flat."

"But what would she do? How could she take care of herself?"

"That would be her problem, then. And stop looking so shocked, please. I'm not a monster. It just so happens that you have to be realistic in cases like this. After all, you can't cure her, can you? When you get right down to it, all you can do is help her to help herself. Isn't that right?"

"I suppose so, but—"

"Of course I'm right. When it comes to handling people, I'm always right. I have a talent for that. Even Mr. Quigley says so, and he ought to know."

"Who's Mr. Quigley?"

"The man in charge of Pop's workers up north. He knows a lot about handling people, too."

It seemed to Evalin, though, that something was wrong about the technique Sue advised. Finally she identified the thing that she thought was wrong. "I don't know," she told Sue. "According to my counselor at Cantwell High, you're not supposed to threaten people just to get your way. According to Miss Rosen, a threat is a type of violence. What you're supposed to do is persuade people, and—"

Sue interrupted with rippling laughter. "Oh, that'll be the day!" Sue cried. "Imagine me taking the time and trouble to persuade the servants to do what I want them to do!"

Evalin thought: my, what a strange girl!

Suddenly Sue stopped laughing. "What did you come here for?" Sue asked, "You want something, of course. Everyone who comes here wants something. Ted comes here because he loves miniature golf. Other kids come to use one of our boats or to swim in the pool or to ride one of the horses. Sometimes it makes me just furious! Nobody ever comes here to give us anything or just to talk to us. Isn't it wonderful to be rich?"

Evalin started to declare hotly that she never came to the Winthrop place for anything. Yet this time she had come for something, definitely! Blushing, she bit her lower lip.

Sue asked with a cruel smile: "Will you have money or jewels or a swim or a game of golf or what?"

Evalin had to shift her gaze from those cat green eyes. She said huskily, ashamedly: "Well, I remembered you folks have a portable wheel chair. I thought I might borrow it. I could write Molly up north, but then she would have to write my folks, and all that would take time. Grammy could use a wheel chair right now, and I don't have enough money to buy one."

"Suppose I told you to go beg somewhere else?"

Evalin considered that, head cocked over her left shoulder. She decided finally that for Grammy she would go beg somewhere else. Why, no girl on earth had ever had a finer grandmother!

And it was *not* horrible to be around sick people, Grammy least of all. And she certainly would *not* abandon Grammy just because Grammy was a problem right now. Glory smoke, families had to stick together no matter what; any fool knew that!

Sue astonished her.

"You bug me," Sue said candidly. "You always have and I guess you always will. And not just because a lot of stupid boys have always made more of a fuss over you than over me. Take right now. Any other girl would have taken the hint and left. I don't want you here. I don't like you, Evalin Mitchell. I never have and I never will, and I don't care if it is terribly rude to tell you that while you're sort of a guest here."

Evalin shrugged. She gripped her skirt to keep it down in a sudden gust of river wind. "As you wish," she said mildly, rather pitying Sue. "But will you tell your mother I'd appreciate the loan of the wheel chair?"

Sue made a strangling sound in her throat. Then she yelled: "It's in the garage! Go ahead and take it! Take Ted Pillsbury, too! I hate you!

Do you hear? I hate you!"

While Evalin stared incredulously, beautiful Sue Winthrop sat down on the grass and began to cry.

Chapter 4

That same afternoon, while Grammy was trying out the wheel chair on the decks of the *Sea
Hawk,* Evalin made the only decision she knew
her conscience would allow her to live with. For
better or worse, she decided, she would help
Grammy on the ferryboat. It was her duty.

Grammy yelled: "Avast there, landlubber;
come here!"

Chuckling, feeling utterly contented now that
she was wearing old denims and an old blouse
again, Evalin loped to the square-ended stern
deck. Grammy gave the portable wheel chair several hard pushes to get up momentum. She then
clamped her right hand down hard on the right
wheel pushing-ring. The chair swung about in a

neat circle. "Girl," Grammy predicted, "I'll be an expert in two hours. Now look. This makes everything different. Anybody who says the *Sea Hawk* will be tied up all summer will be keel-hauled. That means you, Dr. McGrath, Sam Pike, or anybody else. Starting tomorrow morning, the *Sea Hawk* sails at six, and she makes every trip every day during the summer. No sass! Scoot to the house and telephone Mrs. Riley of the *Princess Town Times*. Tell her to print my usual ad beginning tomorrow afternoon."

"Aye, aye, ma'am!"

"And take off those blasted saddle shoes while you're at the house! I'll not have you slipping and skidding around the decks like a Sunday sailor."

Evalin hopefully asked: "Can I go barefooted?"

"Red toenails and all, I suppose? Scandal! I'll have you know, young lady, that when I was your age girls didn't exhibit their toes, and they didn't paint their toenails, either."

"Creeps, what a dull life!"

Grammy startled her. "And while you're in the house," she ordered, "you telephone Dan Wyatt.

Federal 8, 3495. Whether you like him or don't, he's the best of the boys I interviewed last week. Tell him he has a job if he'll still take twenty-five dollars a week."

Rude though it seemed to Evalin, she said quite firmly: "No, ma'am."

"I'll not have mutiny here, girl!"

"Because what will happen?" Evalin asked worriedly. "Dan won't dare tell you to remain in your wheel chair."

"Naturally. The help don't give orders to the boss."

"Then some dreadful day, Grammy, what will happen? You may rupture another blood vessel. Or you may even have a serious stroke. I'm not a doctor's daughter for nothing, Grammy. I may not know the whys of things, but I do know people in your condition can have strokes."

"Make the telephone calls, please."

Instead, Evalin sat down atop the life-preserver bin. She felt this was too important a matter to postpone. This, too, she thought, was a challenge, and certainly it was no more difficult to meet this challenge than it had been to meet the challenge of Sue Winthrop's hatred. One thing she had learned that morning was the value of sticking to your guns to get whatever it was you were after.

Grammy's brow wrinkled. She asked, a bit puzzled: "What is this all about, Mouse? You've always been obedient, I'll give you credit for that."

"I'm the crew," Evalin told her. "Why not, Grammy? You know I love to be on the water! So you steer, and I'll handle the lines and get the cars and people aboard. I have it all figured out. Why, I don't even have to know anything about the engine, because you can tell me what to do when it needs oiling and things like that."

"Rubbish. You don't come down here to work. Why, you don't even know the meaning of work! Running a ferryboat service isn't play, you know."

"Whatever anyone else can do, I can do almost as well."

"Can you, now!"

"In fact," Evalin bragged, "I could even sail

this boat alone if I had to. The only reason I need you along is that I'm a minor."

Grammy rolled her eyes heavenward.

A big idea flashed into Evalin's mind. She said nothing whatsoever to Grammy. She went to the controls behind the wood and glass-paned windscreen. She fiddled with the different levers a moment and breathed a silent prayer that there was enough fuel in the tank below decks. She pushed the starting lever down and fed the engine fuel as it began to sputter and cough in a deep-toned way. Grammy yelled: "You insolent snip!" and then she began to laugh. Grammy, Lord love her, never said or did a thing to interfere. She just sat there while Evalin cast off the bow and stern lines. Not even when Evalin eased the boat forward did Grammy interfere, although the boat was certainly large enough and heavy enough to damage the pier if Evalin did the wrong thing.

Evalin was very careful to do the right things, ransacking her memory feverishly, trying to recall every trick her grandmother used to get the *Sea Hawk* well away from the pier on the port side and the stone jetty on the starboard side. As it developed, however, she really had no need to remember all the tricks. On this historic June afternoon the Princess River lay as smooth as golden glass under the clear, deep blue sky. So with no strong current or driving windcaps to combat, all a girl had to do was steer a straight course and allow the throbbing engine to do the rest.

Grammy nodded once the pier and the jetty had been left behind. "Couldn't have done better myself," she conceded.

"Care to take over, ma'am?"

"Why?"

"Well, you know darned well I can't *dock* this thing!"

"Nonsense. Haven't I said over and over that you have Murdock blood in you? A Murdock can do anything on the water. Sailing's in our blood."

But Grammy did roll her chair behind the windscreen and did take over the controls. She did it with such shining eyes that Evalin was glad she had thought of quitting while she was still ahead.

Now from the *Sea Hawk* came a deep-throated

honk. A bell was clanged, and the fat ferryboat picked up speed. All along the shore, the Saturday afternoon picnickers and sun-bathers waved, and about a hundred feet farther on some fellows on the riverfront lawn of Town Park sank to their knees and clasped their hands supplicatingly and howled requests for a free ride.

"I don't like boys," Grammy confided. "They are too noisy, for one thing, and they're too mischievous, for another. You stay away from the boys until you have some sense behind that pretty face."

"Never!"

"Orders!"

Evalin pulled a deck chair behind the windscreen. It began to feel like old times. Often during the nine years she had been coming to spend her summers on the Eastern Shore of Maryland, she had had good chats with Grammy right there near the controls. She had learned much from those chats. And ah, the lovely scenery she had looked at. She wondered now why she had thought last week that Birch Corners was the prettiest little town on the Eastern Shore. Look at Princess Town stretched for a mile along the river front! Great mansions and park-like lawns. Cute slate-roofed cottages and bungalows that reminded you of New England. Great horse chestnut trees everywhere, and stately old elms, too. And dearest of all, three white churches with tall, needle-pointed spires, each church standing in the perfect spot to complete the lovely picture.

"Why won't you stay away from boys?" Grammy asked.

"Antisocial behavior, Grammy. Anyway, such orders are plain insulting. When you give such orders, you imply a girl is a dimwit. Well, I have news for you. I'm not a dimwit, believe it or not. Sure, I love to dance and things like that. I can even become very excited about a good-looking boy lugging a football for a touchdown on a crisp autumn afternoon. But I don't go steadily with any one boy and I don't swoon over any one boy. In fact, all things considered, I'm pretty sensible."

Grammy swung the boat a few degrees to port. The *Sea Hawk* curved away from the shore. A sea gull came along and invited itself to bum a ride. The gull landed on a railing up forward. Because it looked smaller than most of the gulls you saw around Princess Town, Evalin wondered if this was the bird she had rooted for one day in the marshland.

Grammy said suddenly, "Let me tell you something, Mouse. And I won't be preaching, either. Just let me say this. There's a time and a place for all experience. There's a time for thinking only about yourself, and there's a time for thinking about others. There's also a time for a girl to think pretty darned seriously about boys, and then about one particular boy. But that time isn't at your age, because at your age you haven't had a chance to get to know people very well. Sure, you can handle me in a way, and you can handle your parents in a way. But what does that mean? You can handle us only because we love you, because we won't take advantage of your inexperience. Catch?"

"It's all right, Grammy."

"What's all right?"

"I learned my lesson two weeks ago when I saw

my grades. I was awfully ashamed. All right. Maybe I'll give some of these fellows a bad time, because I can't always be perfect. But regardless of what Mom told you, I won't run wild."

Grammy looked at her fiercely, in a proud way Evalin knew she would never forget. "You think I don't know that?" Grammy asked. "You have Murdock blood in you. A Murdock can be trusted to be sensible. It just so happens that I reminded your mother of that fact."

Evalin wanted to kiss her at that moment. She felt close to Grammy, suddenly. You could talk to Grammy. Regardless of her bark, Grammy could be darned understanding!

Now the light changed on the Princess River. In midstream, you could feel the surge of the current flowing west, and if you looked straight overside you could see that the water was a deeper blue than the water closer to shore. The wind there seemed fresher, all the world seemed cleaner. Best of all was the delicious feeling of being utterly alone in the sea world with Grammy.

Grammy said, "Sue Winthrop telephoned while

you were bringing the wheel chair. She apologizes for what she said to you."

Evalin shrugged.

"Mouse, I'm grateful for the wheel chair, of course. I'm grateful for your offer to help run this ferryboat. I don't need charity, though."

Evalin went a bit tense.

"Still," Grammy said, "if it will help you to settle down a bit, you may help me run this ferryboat."

Evalin's mouth fell open.

But when her eyes met Grammy's eyes, Evalin suddenly understood that her grandmother had pride, and that her pride just would not allow her to accept what she considered to be charity.

Evalin said, eyes sparkling: "Aye, aye, ma'am."

Chapter 5

Evalin felt less pleased with herself at four o'clock the following morning. All her life she had been a late starter, a girl who awakened practically by inches and who lingered long in bed while her mind and her emotions slowly and resentfully accepted the fact a new day had come. It was not that life bored her, as Molly sometimes claimed, for once she had begun her day she always hated to end it. But Evalin did like to be comfortable and she did like to set her own living pace, and it always seemed to her in the morning dark and cool and quiet that it was downright brutal of people like Molly to expect a girl to leave warm feathers and pleasant dreams before her bones and her spirit were quite ready to. On one memorable occasion, Evalin had told Molly this. Big, brawny, gray-uniformed Molly had been quite indignant. Molly had predicted huffily that a few more words like that would cost Dr. and Mrs. Mitchell her services. "Just you remember," Molly had said, "that I don't have to stay here to be insulted." But of course Molly had not resigned her position. In a sense, Molly was one of the family by now, and how could a person resign from her family? So on through the years Molly had come to Evalin's bedroom at six-thirty every morning to get her up, and on through the years Evalin had continued her protests. One of the reasons she had always loved spending her summers with her grandmother was that she had always been allowed to get up when she chose. But now she heard the alarm clock! Why, the moon was still shining! Probably every ghost and hobgoblin in old Princess Town was still walking about, enjoying the damp, cold air!

Somehow Evalin forced herself out of bed. Barefooted, shivering in her lilac Capri pajamas, she picked her way across the dark room to one of the dormer windows. The outdoors looked quite unappealing to her, despite the lovely streamers of moonlight on the murmuring Princess River. When Evalin remembered that her grandmother had been getting up at that hour for years and years, she was appalled. She would have to do something about *that*. It was utterly disgraceful that a fine old lady like her grandmother had to get up so early just to earn beans for the old pot!

Grammy yelled down below: "Hit the deck, Mouse; hit the deck!"

Evalin told her to stop frightening the ghosts and hobgoblins. She had a shower. She did her room. By then breakfast was ready, a working girl's breakfast consisting of oatmeal and boiled eggs, half a grapefruit and toast and milk. Fully dressed, wasting no time on idle talk, while they ate Grammy outlined a daily schedule she had worked out sometime during the night. The housework would *not* be done before the first trip at six o'clock. "There's time enough to do that," Grammy said, "between noon and four. We eat lunch, we tidy up, then the next two hours are yours. Understood?"

Grinning, Evalin said: "Aye, aye, ma'am."

"All day Saturday is yours, too," Grammy went on. "We make only four trips on Saturdays and Sundays, so you can be spared a full day. Sam Pike will relieve you on Saturday, and he'll relieve me on Sunday."

"Why not the other way around? Mr. Pike and I could clean the boat on Saturday so it'll look nice for the Sunday churchgoers."

"Because I'll *not* have you go home in September looking as if I'd worked you half to death!"

"Just the same—"

"You never argue with the captain, Mouse. That happens to be a law of life. Whoever your boss is, you listen and you obey."

"Well, if Molly can argue with me, why can't I argue with you?"

"Very simple. You aren't Molly's boss; your father is. And you stop reminding me that you have a servant at home! If you're going to be a working girl, then be one."

"Molly isn't a servant," Evalin told her indignantly. "She happens to be a housekeeper and a part of our family, which isn't the same thing as a servant at all."

Grammy could not be drawn into a discussion about *that,* however. With business on her mind, Grammy was all business. Well before Evalin was ready to go to work, Grammy had her out of the house, hosing down the decks of the *Sea Hawk.* By then the sky was a beautiful mellow pink shot through with fascinating shades of green and blue. Faithfully reflecting the sky, the river reminded Evalin of stained glass. But the river appeared even lovelier than stained glass to her because it was quiveringly alive. It was quite difficult for Evalin to keep her mind on her chore. Too many interesting things were going on. A kingfisher went screeching by, taking the air route to Carter Hollow across the river. Menhaden came leaping from the water to show their silvered sides before they flopped back to the river and disappeared. A great school of minnows went rushing by the bow of the *Sea Hawk,* ruffling the water and leaving lacy foam behind them. Then a car came along, and who should be at the wheel of the car but Dr. McGrath! Dr. McGrath said, grinning, "Your folks should see you now. Isn't that water rather cold?"

"Probably I'll never survive this summer," Eva-lin predicted. "But Grammy says the only way to hose down the decks is to roll your pants up and take off your shoes and socks and splash away."

Another car came rolling onto the stout pier and was halted inches from Dr. McGrath's. Eva-lin got her hose rolled up and put away and let the men drive their cars aboard. If the *Sea Hawk* were loaded carefully, she knew, it could accommodate nine average-sized passenger cars and a couple of trucks, and she made certain that the two cars were driven well forward before she put the chocks under the wheels and let the men stop the car engines.

The second driver was a stranger to Evalin, a short, rather stout man whose stomach bulged out and seemed to hang over his belt buckle. He refused the single-passage ticket she offered him.

"Kid," he said, "meet a new steady customer. Talk about a relief to have the *Sea Hawk* back in service again! I'll have the thirty-trip book of tickets, please."

"Round trips, sir?"

"Round trips."

He took two twenty-dollar bills from his wallet. Evalin had to hustle into the house for his change, and the sight of her bare, wet feet and rolled up pants was too much for Grammy. Grammy whooped with laughter. "What a ship-shape sailor *you* are," Grammy teased. "Mouse, I promote you to admiral."

"Do admirals push wheel chairs, do you think?"

"I demote you."

So Evalin pushed the wheel chair up the ramp to the pier and along the pier to the gangplank. There, with the men looking on interestedly, Grammy took over, pushing herself along with quite vigorous strokes. Dr. McGrath, it developed, had the privilege of riding without charge whenever he was making a professional call on someone in Carter Hollow. He argued the matter amiably, but Grammy flatly refused his fifty cents. Grammy went on to the controls behind the windscreen and got the motor started and tooted the whistle three times. Tooting the whistle ten minutes before a sailing was good practise, as Evalin discovered. Suddenly five cars came driving to the pier. Then a truck rumbled up, and this was a two-dollar truck. Finally, about three minutes before sailing time, about a dozen workmen came along and flipped Evalin their quarters.

And business grew better as the morning advanced. The proceeds for the first round trip, exclusive of the thirty-trip ticket book Evalin had sold, amounted to sixteen dollars. The seven o'clock sailing for Carter Hollow again was made with a full compliment of cars and trucks, but the sailing from Carter Hollow at seven-thirty was even more profitable: nothing but trucks on the decks and fully thirty foot passengers scattered all over the boat. During the ten-minute wait before the third sailing from Princess Town, Grammy announced that the morning rush was about over.

"The first two round trips are the big ones of the morning," she explained. "That's one of the reasons we have to be punctual for those. Folks have to get to work or deliver things before the stores and shops open. Actually, the only reason we make three more round trips in the morning is that a lot of shoppers like to hit the stores around nine and ten o'clock. That way, they get about five hours in either Carter Hollow or Princess Town before they have to head home to cook chow and such."

But on this particular morning, at least, there was no shortage of cars or foot passengers. A big crowd of boy scouts climbed aboard the Sea Hawk for the eight o'clock sailing. Evalin sold forty tickets at twenty cents apiece, and was sure that she had missed some of the kids. The boys were amused by her attempt to count noses as Grammy sent the *Sea Hawk* pushing once more across the river to Carter Hollow. One, a first-class scout, insisted there were only thirty scouts aboard and that she owed some of the kids refunds. Then, horribly, one boy who turned out not to be a scout at all became quite rude.

"Look," he said. "If I told you I paid, then I paid. Anyway, why don't you get wise to yourself and go back home? This was supposed to be Dan Wyatt's job. It was all fixed until the rich Evalin Mitchell decided to play at being a working girl. How does it feel to take the bread out of a guy's mouth?"

It was such a sudden, savage attack that Evalin was jarred speechless. She could only stare at the boy with hurt, stricken eyes.

He laughed jeeringly. "What's the matter, rich girl?" he asked. "Can't you stand the truth? Well, you'll have to learn, all right. Just wait until all the town kids hear what you've done. We don't need kids coming down here to take jobs away from us, I'll tell you that."

A couple of the scouts pushed between Evalin and the boy. One scout said he knew darned well that Tom Crowell had not paid his fare, and finally the scouts shamed him into doing so. But he never gave Evalin the money. He took a quarter from his pocket and flung it contemptuously to the deck. He laughed as Evalin scrambled after it. "Boy," he said, "you sure love money, don't you?"

That, Evalin decided, was quite enough. She let the quarter remain on deck. She marched over to the rude Mr. Tom Crowell and told him he would either hand her the quarter and mind his manners or find another way to get back home from Carter Hollow.

Grammy surprised her. Her face stern, her eyes blazing, Grammy called: "Evalin, pick up that quarter and then come here!"

Perfectly furious, Evalin obeyed.

Loud enough for everyone to hear, Grammy snapped, "I'll not have you fighting with my customers, thank you. That's an order, too!"

"But . . ."

Grammy turned her attention back to her steering. Because they were nearing the Carter Hollow pier, Evalin kept her tongue still and went forward to flip a line up and around a mooring bitt. Mr. Tom Crowell yelled: "Ten to one she goofs!" It was one time Evalin did not goof, however, and all the boy scouts cheered.

After everyone had disembarked, Grammy grinned. "Easy does it," she advised. "Listen to me a second. We run this boat to make money, and Tom Crowell's quarter is just as spendable as anybody else's money. You remember that. In business, you're not personal. What you should have done was walk away from him.

Evalin demanded hotly: "Did you hear what he said?"

"Yup."

"Well?"

"Fighting with Tom Crowell won't prove to anyone you didn't steal Dan Wyatt's job."

"But all I'm trying to do is help you, Grammy."

"Sure. And most of the kids, even Tom, will understand that if you give them the chance. But if you throw your weight around, you'll get everybody angry. Then what will happen? Angry people don't take the time to understand anyone."

Evalin said haughtily: "Well, if I have to humor the likes of Tom Crowell to win his understanding, he can just drop dead."

But more people came aboard, and Evalin had to go forward again to supervise the parking of cars and to collect the fares. In her reaction to the unpleasantness of the public insult, Evalin was coldly businesslike. Once the last homeward trip of the morning had begun, Evalin went to the galley and remained there until Grammy had eased the *Sea Hawk* close to the Princess Town pier. Evalin tied the boat to the pier and then went straight into the house to telephone Dan Wyatt and clue him in on her reasons for taking the job. Dan, though, never gave her a chance to explain. "Kiddo," Dan said, "you'll be sorry." And he broke the connection with a bang.

Chapter 6

On July first it became painfully clear to Evalin that the enmity of Tom Crowell and Dan Wyatt had to be taken seriously. After lunch that Wednesday, while she was walking to the post office for the mail, Evalin met Doris Craddock and Sandra Buell, two of her favorite town girls. Evalin gaily linked arms with them and suggested they go mooch a crabmeat snack at the crab cannery near the marshland. Sandra looked at Doris, and Doris rolled her big gray eyes. Pink-faced with sudden embarrassment, Sandra presently said that crabmeat bored her. Evalin had to laugh. "I'd hate to have to pay for all the crabmeat you can eat," she teased Sandra. "How in the world do you keep that beautiful figure?"

Sandra did an astonishing thing. As they neared Morgan's Alley, Sandra whooped: "Run, geese, home!"

Off the two girls scooted, so Evalin had to follow. They went through cobblestoned Morgan's Alley and then along the red brick sidewalks of Colonial Way to Wisteria Lane. When they had reached Sandra's cute yellow-shingled home, Sandra ordered, "Make like dignified ladies." Self-consciously dignified, they went around the house to the lawn swing in the rear yard. Sandra got milk and chocolate-chip cookies from the kitchen. "Made the cookies myself," Sandra bragged. "Chew and rue."

A cardinal flew into the yard, a sassy creature possessed of a flashing yellow bill. The cardinal landed in the smoke tree to the left of the white classic bird bath. His red seemed particularly intense against the rich green leaves. His whistling was so downright engaging that Doris tossed half a cookie toward the tree. The cardinal refused the cookie, however. He darted to the bird bath and took three sips of water, then streaked on again to goodness knew where. Sandra said, "My, how I hate to see food wasted!" Sandra retrieved the half-cookie and popped it into her mouth.

Suddenly Doris asked Sandra: "Why are we wasting time? Do you ask Evalin the big question, or do I?

Evalin looked from one face to the other, intrigued.

It was Sandra who asked the big question. "What's the feud about, Evalin?" she asked. "At the Strawberry Goo the other evening, Tom Crowell and Dan Wyatt laid down the law. All the kids of Princess Town are supposed to snub you. Anyone who doesn't snub you will be sorry. Why? There isn't a girl in town who isn't dumb-founded. Why, you practically ruled the roost last year!"

Evalin was too dumbfounded herself to answer.

Doris said unhappily, "Nobody wants to snub you, of course, least of all Sandra and me. Candid-ly, you're the only summer girl I've ever liked. Take right now, for example. You're not too proud to be seen with us. The way girls like Sue Winthrop behave, you'd think we were plain dirt. So before I snub you, I'd like to know what your side of the story is."

Now a turkey buzzard came into view, soaring so high on practically motionless wings it seemed smaller than it was. Evalin loved the appearance of the bird against the deep blue sky. She wished rather childishly that she could be up there with it, soaring wild and free.

"Did you or didn't you steal Dan Wyatt's job?" Sandra asked. "If you did, Evalin, it was mean. Dan wants to go to college, and his folks can't afford to send him, so he needs work."

"Of course I didn't! Why should I? Do you honestly believe, either of you, that I came to Maryland to work?"

"Well, how come you are working, then?"

"It's very simple, really. Grammy needs my help. Anyway, there never was a job opening as such. This happens to be an emergency. When Grammy is well enough to operate the boat without help, the job won't exist any more."

Doris gave Sandra a quick glance. "That must be why Dan's so angry," Doris conjectured. "Dan wants just a summer job, remember? The ferry-boat job would have been perfect for him."

Evalin almost asked how Dan had expected her grandmother to earn enough money to pay him a salary. It occurred to Evalin in time, however, that her grandmother would not thank her for telling people money was a problem just now.

"Too bad about Dan's needs," Evalin said sarcastically. "It would have been perfect for me just to loaf around all summer, but you don't hear me complaining."

Sandra asked: "Well, why not quit, then? You'll be happy, and Dan will be happy."

Now both girls were looking at Evalin in a way they had never looked at her before: a bit resentfully, a bit disappointedly, a bit scornfully. Suddenly, in some way, their eyes conveyed the message that Evalin had reached a crossroads in her relationship with them. She knew deep down that if in any way her answer displeased them, their attitude toward her would change drastically.

"Actually," Evalin said carefully, "Grammy needs a boss as much as a helper. She needs someone to make her stay in that wheel chair. How could Dan do that? It's all I can do to make her follow Dr. McGrath's orders, and I'm family."

Doris Craddock declared: "That's ridiculous! No one has to be bossed into following a doctor's orders! Why would an adult pay a doctor for advice that will save her life and then go ahead and ignore that advice?"

Doris stood up, quite indignant now, her little chin quivering, her lovely eyes flashing. She said to Sandra, "Well, if that's the best excuse Evalin can think of, count me out. Really, I'm not a dunce!"

Sandra looked at Evalin and said pleadingly: "Try again, honey, will you? Listen, maybe you don't understand something you should understand. This is a small town, a difficult place for kids to find work. Well, a lot of us are poor and a lot of us need our summer jobs. So, naturally, we resent it when a summer girl comes down here and takes a job she really doesn't need. You'd resent it, too, if you were in our position, wouldn't you?"

Evalin said flatly, "I've told you the truth."

"It doesn't make sense to me, either, Evalin. I'm sorry, but it just doesn't."

Evalin caught her breath.

Sandra went on somewhat sadly, "Why should I risk being ostracized by the crowd to enjoy the company of a girl I can't believe? That wouldn't be sensible, would it?"

"But—"

Sandra said harshly: "Scoot, Evalin. It so happens I'm like everybody else here. I value my friendship with Tom and Dan and all the others too much to lose it for the sake of a summer girl who wants to play at being a working girl."

Nor would either girl listen to another word! Both went into the house and slammed the door pointedly behind them. All Evalin could do was leave.

It was even worse at the post office. As always, a gang of kids had gathered before the brick, vine-hung building to chat a while before going home with the noon mail. In the past, Evalin had always been welcomed quite cheerily by the kids, as if they considered her to be one of the town girls. This day, however, a girl booed her as Evalin came along the walk, and all the kids joined in. Three fellows actually barred the brick sidewalk to force Evalin to walk either on the road or the post office lawn. For a moment, Evalin had no idea what to do. This being her first experience with that sort of thing, she did not know whether to make the enforced detour or to compel the three boys to halt her physically. Finally, almost ill with anger, she decided that if she were bluffed now she would be bullied whenever and wherever she showed her face in town.

Head up, shoulders squared, Evalin neither took the detour nor stopped walking. The booing stopped. A girl cried out: "Don't let her past!" A couple of adults near the post office entrance noticed what was going on, and one of the woman called: "You kids behave!"

When she was quite near the boys, Evalin looked from one face to the next and asked sweetly: "What happens when you need to use the *Sea Hawk*?"

The boy in the middle, a fellow who *had* to use the *Sea Hawk* every afternoon, gave her an angry look. "Just try to keep me off!" he said grimly. "Just try."

Queerly, the whole thing suddenly reminded Evalin of a scene she had witnessed the preceding December back home in Cantwell. Several of the girls in the sophomore class had taken a dislike to a freshman girl and had tried to prevent the girl from entering the locker room without their specific permission. The freshman girl had solved the problem quite brilliantly. She had said to one of the sophs: "Do you behave, or do I have to tattle about you know what?"

It had been a dreadful thing to threaten, really, but it had worked!

Evalin said to the boy in the middle, "I promise to repay all bullying in kind, and I always keep my promises."

He almost stood his ground, but at the last second he gave way. Doing her best to conceal her trembles of relief, Evalin swept on to the post office before someone could think up some other strategy.

Mrs. Locatelli gave her a warm smile behind her barred window. "Letter from your folks," Mrs. Locatelli announced. "Do you have a stamp collection?"

"Nope. Dolls."

"At your age? You're joking!"

Evalin took the Thailand stamp off the envelope and gave it to Mrs. Locatelli. In no mood to explain why she collected dolls, she went to a wooden bench near the windows and took out the thin, crackly pages of the letter and read them hungrily.

The first part of the letter, she discovered, had been written by her father. He told her that Dr. McGrath had sent him a complete diagnosis of Grammy's problems and that it was too bad they had not known of these problems a month or so sooner. Anyway, her father wrote, Dr. McGrath was a good doctor, so everything that could be done for Grammy was being done.

"And behold the nurse!" her father wrote on. "At the risk of spoiling you, I must say I'm quite proud of the way you've stepped into the breach. It's always disappointing to end up working hard when all along you expected to be the idle belle of the Princess River. But family is family, isn't it? Sure it is! So do your best for Grammy, no matter what, and perhaps I'll kiss you come September 20th.

Sue Winthrop came into the post office, quite lovely this afternoon in a yellow sports ensemble. Sue gave her a wave that seemed a taunt to Evalin, but Evalin found it impossible to resent the taunt.

Sue dropped lightly to a seat beside Evalin. "And how's dear Mrs. Murdock?" Sue asked. "I must come see for myself one of these days. But I'm so terribly busy, you know. Boys, boys, boys."

"Grammy appreciated the chair, Sue. So did I. And you must come see her soon, because you have a free trip coming to you."

"I saw what happened outside. You're a peculiar girl, did you know? I could never have done what you did."

"Had I stopped to think about it, I guess I couldn't have done it, either. I became angry, I guess. Just because I'm helping my grandmother, I'm to be snubbed."

"Well, they do have a point, you know. And we summer girls have still another point. You certainly aren't helping our prestige by working on that ferryboat! Even my mother was shocked when she heard about your job. She said girls in our class have no business working."

"Well, if it's all right for my folks to help in Thailand, why isn't it all right for me to help Grammy here?"

"It isn't as if she couldn't afford to hire Dan, is it?"

There was an eager look in Sue Winthrop's eyes that Evalin did not like. Instinctively, Evalin knew that whatever she told Sue would be used by Sue in some way or another for her own advantage.

"Grammy needs help," Evalin said evasively. "If I were sick, Grammy would help me. Isn't that what families are for?"

But a boy came in and, squealing and laughing, Sue went over to him. Evalin went back to her letter, the part her mother had written. Way down near the last page her mother, too, referred to the help she was giving Grammy. "The difference between immaturity and maturity," her mother wrote, "is the difference between perceiving and not perceiving responsibility to others. I salute you, Duck. You get ruby earrings when I return home."

Evalin had to blink hard to keep from crying. Why, those earrings were her mother's most treasured possession!

Chapter 7

On Saturday, not eager to spend her day off being snubbed in Princess Town, Evalin borrowed her grandmother's sailboat and headed early across the Princess River to the Bishop estate on Heron Creek. Evalin had a good sail. The wind was not too strong, nor did it shift directions so often she had to remain quite alert at the tiller. Holding the sail line with her right hand and keeping the tiller steady with her left knee, Evalin was able to relax and to enjoy herself with a minimum of work. She was particularly interested in the antics of a barnyard skate she saw about halfway across the river. The skate was moving along in most leisurely fashion only about a foot or so below the surface. Its movements were accomplished by means of its sides, each side fluttering as if it were a wing. Evalin had always associated skates with river mud; hence she was quite surprised to see this particular skate "flying" along as if it, too, had decided to have an outing. She wondered about its destination. She hoped it would not eventually settle down in the mud of Heron Creek. Say she went swimming with MaryAnn Bishop. Say her naked foot came down on the barb the skate carried in its tail. Two cripples aboard one ferryboat would be one cripple too many! And how humiliating it would be if Dan Wyatt had to be hired after all!

A hail interrupted Evalin's troubled thoughts. She discovered that while her mind had been churning, the catboat had carried her almost to the entrance of Heron Creek. And there on the little islet in the mouth of the creek stood a girl who certainly should have known better than to set foot on that squishy land in the first place. Evalin altered course to approach the islet somewhat against the wind. Knowing that the water around the islet was shallow, Evalin pulled up the centerboard of the catboat and moored it carefully into place. It required some deft sailing to keep the catboat from drifting off course once the stabilizing influence of the centerboard had been sacrificed. The girl on the islet seemed to understand that and said absolutely nothing whatsoever to distract Evalin as she inched closer and closer to the shore.

It was done!

Hardly had the boat gently bumped on something fairly solid when the girl scrambled aboard, a wild creature indeed in patched levis and a dirty T-shirt, her red hair disheveled, her bare legs and feet daubed with sea mud and slime. Once she was aboard, the girl picked up one of the oars and poled the catboat away from the islet. "Starboard ho!" the girl ordered. "Mind the rocks now!"

Evalin obediently swung to starboard. As the wind hit the sail, the girl scrambled amidships and let the centerboard drop back into the water. At once, the drifting stopped and the catboat surged ahead. The girl came back to the stern and sat down on the port gunwale and stuck both legs into the water almost up to her knees.

The girl said, "Thanks."

Evalin said, "You're welcome."

"Boat drifted away," the girl said. "Fool thing for a boat to do. You ever notice boats do lots of fool things? That's a funny thing about boats."

"Well, people do fool things, too, I've noticed. For example, they forget to moor their boats when they should. Which way did it drift?"

"Choptank way."

Evalin swung the boat west.

The girl understood and smiled shyly. "Real nice of you. Without a boat you can't do much around here. In case you don't know, I'm Jamie Holloway."

"I'm Evalin Mitchell."

"Oh, I know who you are. How's Cap?"

"Cap?"

"Mrs. Murdock, silly. I always call her Cap. You tell Cap any time she needs me, just to call Jamie."

Then, if you please, Jamie calmly took a sandwich from Evalin's picnic hamper and went up to the bow to chomp away while she kept her eyes darting every whichway for the boat that had drifted off.

Oddly enough, Evalin neither resented the theft of her sandwich nor grew nervous over the prospect of having Jamie aboard for what might be hours. Actually, she found it quite interesting to have met the "wild girl of Princess Town" at last. What a beautiful girl she was! That hair of Jamie's was practically a living flame! And behold her profile and her trim figure! Put Jamie into a sudsy bath for an hour, then dress her in nice clothes and do her hair, and Jamie would be the honey bee of Princess Town, all right, just buzz, buzz, buzzing along as Sue Winthrop longed to but never would!

Suddenly Jamie laughed. She came back to the stern, so quick and electric with energy she reminded Evalin of a wild fox she had once seen running along a stone fence in New Hampshire. Jamie asked, "How come you aren't snoopy? How come you didn't ask me why I was on that island?"

"Never thought of it," Evalin fibbed.

"You catch croakers from that island, that's why I was there," Jamie explained. "If you slice and fry croakers, they're mighty good eating. If you roll the slices in cornmeal, you can't eat anything nicer."

"I prefer oysters," Evalin told her. "Not cooked, though. I went out with some oystermen one October. We tonged the oysters up from the beds, and one man opened them as fast as I could eat them. Nice and cold and tangy."

Jamie nodded. She pointed off to their right at a pole sticking up from the river. "Best place to steal 'em is right there. Only in months with an 'r' in them, though."

"Why's that?"

Jamie shrugged.

They sailed on a quarter-hour or so before Jamie spoke again. Evalin rather welcomed the silence because now she was sailing a stretch of river fairly new to her. Once they had rounded

Hooke Point the river narrowed and deepened and picked up speed. Here and there the knife edges of rocks showed above the water, and around these rocks was eternal foam, swishing and thundering most dramatically. To avoid the rocks, Evalin had to swing to port. Jamie pointed to some bitterns standing on a lonely spit of land, and Evalin aimed the boat toward them, thinking the girl wanted a closer look. To her surprise, she spotted a creek running deep and green between two pretty stands of birch trees. Jamie said: "Pirate's Cove, where we live."

Amazingly, Jamie jumped overboard. Startled, Evalin began to swing the boat around, but Jamie called tauntingly from the water: "Tricked you! Tricked you!" Then off Jamie swam with powerful strokes to the shore.

Evalin counted aloud to ten. But she was still so angry when she reached ten that she felt tempted to go after the girl and give her a tongue lashing. Two things happened, though, to prevent that. First, a cracking sound came from the shore, as if someone had fired a rifle. Then who but Dan

Wyatt should come out of the cottage farther up the creek, and Jamie's brother with him! Not in any mood to tangle with both Dan and Jamie, Evalin swung her boat around and headed for the second time that morning for the Bishop estate on Heron Creek.

Quite huffy about having been kept waiting, MaryAnn spouted for two minutes on the subject of manners. But Evalin's excuse was finally considered acceptable. Intrigued, MaryAnn waved Evalin to the picnic place already laid out under the oaks. "I met Jamie once," MaryAnn confided. Suddenly there Jamie was. I said hello, and she jumped ninety feet in the air, and did she take off when she hit the ground!"

"I resent being tricked, darn it! If she needed a lift, why didn't she just say so?"

"The local kids don't like her, that's why."

"Well, they wouldn't let her be marooned there, would they?"

MaryAnn rolled her snapping black eyes. "Lots of kids think she's insane, you know."

"Rubbish."

"How do you know?"

"Just once, will you stop asking me how I know this or that?"

"Temper!"

Evalin got the message and smiled apologetically. "Sorry. Darn it, I'm upset. And why should I be? Why should I let any of the kids around here bug me? I've done nothing horrible. If they want to be silly, let them be silly."

MaryAnn got the food out of Evalin's hamper. She looked each sandwich over very suspiciously, as if sure that Evalin had included egg salad sandwiches, which happened to be MaryAnn's pet dislike. "Actually," MaryAnn said thoughtfully, "your problem isn't the local kids but Sue Winthrop. How come Sue hates you?"

"I didn't know she did."

"She does. For instance, she came here yesterday and proposed that all the summer kids join the Evalin Mitchell Freeze Club."

Evalin was flabbergasted.

"Oh, I told her to drop dead," MaryAnn announced. "But if I know Sue, she'll get a lot of the summer kids to drop you. Sue can be pretty darned persuasive when she calls you a traitor to your class. Also, I think Sue is a little jealous because Ted rather admires you."

"Does he, now!"

MaryAnn chuckled. "Say, maybe you'd better not be angry with Jamie! Jamie's a girl who can tell you that the freeze doesn't hurt as much as you think it does. I guess the local kids have been snubbing Jamie and her brother for years."

"Really?"

MaryAnn nodded solemnly. "I'm afraid so, honey. Now you listen to me a second. All the years you've been coming down here you've behaved as if the Eastern Shore kids are special kids. They're not. They can be just as mean as kids in your own home town. What they've been doing to Jamie and what they're trying to do to you is proof of that. So if you ask me, you're not missing much even if they snub you all summer long."

"But Sandra and Doris and—"

"Pfui! I have news for you. Your grandmother telephoned about an hour ago. Guess what Sandra and Doris and Tom Crowell are doing right this minute. They're picketing the *Sea Hawk!* Actually! They have signs saying you're unfair to kids who need their jobs. See what lovely friends you have?"

Chapter 8

Grammy was disinclined to take the picketing seriously. Although at least twenty boys and girls came that evening to picket the ferryboat pier and to chant, "Unfair! Unfair!" Grammy sat unconcernedly in the living room, checking her receipts for the week. "The more I study these figures," Grammy announced, "the better I like them. Give me five weeks like this last one, and I may even be able to pay you a nickel a week."

Dutifully, Evalin smiled.

"Mouse," Grammy ordered, "stop peeking out that window. Peeking won't change things, nor will worry change them, either."

"It upsets me," Evalin confessed. "I don't care

if they want to snub me. After all, I'll be leaving in September. But if they drive all your customers away, what will you do?"

"They won't."

Evalin wished she could feel as sure about that as Grammy appeared to be. The presence of Sue Winthrop on the picket line was particularly disturbing to Evalin. She knew that poor, jealous, frustrated Sue was fully capable of doing just about anything to win the genuine friendship of the local boys and girls. And Sue definitely was not an opponent to dismiss lightly! Sue was clever enough to hatch some darned unpleasant schemes. Sue was rich enough to support the ferryboat boycotters with refreshments, and she could even keep reluctant pickets on the line by promising to give parties and other rewards to those who stuck until the bitter end. Moreover, Sue was just bored and restless enough to keep the boycott going simply for kicks!

"How about checkers?" Grammy asked. "Mr. Pike won't be here before eight."

"Would you mind if I didn't play?"

"Playing is better than fuming."

"Well, I can't just lie down and let them walk all over you, Grammy. Actually, this is my fight. All those pickets are around my age, and I certainly ought to be able to handle them."

"Rubbish."

Evalin went outdoors anyway. For a time she sat under one of the apple trees, just studying the boys and girls marching back and forth before the pier entrance. Then she discovered that Sue had sat down on the pier to cool off in the sweet river breeze. Evalin joined Sue there, ignoring the boos of the pickets and a comically haughty Winthrop glare. Not at all nervous, Evalin looped her arms over her knees and gazed thoughtfully at the river. "This is the best time of day," she told Sue. "Have you ever noticed? Suddenly all the world seems to change a few minutes after sunset. Everything seems quieter. Everything turns peaceful. Dad says it happens the same way in Thailand. I suppose, actually, it happens the same way all over the world."

"Why does he go to Thailand every summer?"

"He likes the people. He says they need his help. Also, he gets to do a lot of surgery. Up in Cantwell he teaches most of the time, so he needs to do surgery in the summer to keep in training, sort of."

Sue nodded as if she understood. But it was obvious she was not particularly interested in either Dr. Mitchell or the need that existed in Thailand. Sue darted a quick glance at the picket line. "I'm very proud of those kids," Sue confided. "There's a dance at the recreation hall this evening, but nobody begged off."

"They march well," Evalin told her. "I think a couple of the girls are getting pretty tired, but who wouldn't after hours of that?"

"Tomorrow we'll be better organized," Sue promised maliciously. "That's to say, provided you don't surrender this evening."

Evalin had to laugh. "You may relax," she told Sue. "I really won't surrender this evening."

"Frankly," Sue confided, "I'd love to keep this going at least a week. It's amazing how popular you can become if you just side with the peasants.

I have three invitations to the Yacht Club Dance next Saturday. And on Sunday, believe it or not, I'm to be second sailor in Ted's catboat. Guess who'll come in first?"

Evalin said, shocked, "They're not peasants! Really, why do you say such things?"

"Pah! I could hire any one of them for practically buttons a week. I could make any one of them jump through a hoop if I wanted to. Golly, what an odd upbringing you've had! Facts are facts, and you ought to accept them as such."

From the picket line came a call for Sue. It was Doris Craddock. Doris was limping, as if she had developed a painful blister. But Doris was still in the line, loyally performing what she clearly considered to be her duty.

Sue said matter-of-factly, "Let her suffer awhile. According to Mr. Quigley, it's good for little people to suffer. Did I tell you that Mr. Quigley is in charge of all Dad's workers up north?"

"You ought to be ashamed!"

"I'm not."

Evalin wished she could understand Sue. The

girl had many likable qualities. But she had this cruelty in her makeup, too. Why?

Sue smiled very prettily. "We're going to squash you, Evalin," Sue vowed. "It may take some time, but sooner or later we'll force you off the *Sea Hawk* and make you come crawling to us. Isn't that interesting? Now ask me why we're going to squash you?"

Evalin shrugged, pretending a nonchalance she certainly did not possess. "Oh," she answered, "I'd guess you want to squash me because I've always been more popular than you. Glory smoke, that's obvious! I never had to bribe kids to come see me or include me in their activities. Right?"

"Wrong. It's because you're a traitor to your social group."

"Pfui."

Then Evalin got a wonderful break. Who should come along, looking puzzled by the pickets, but Ted Pillsbury? Ted came onto the pier and asked outright: "What gives?"

Sue said irritably, "I told you all about it, Ted. This snip here has stolen a job from Dan Wyatt.

We're trying to give her the message we think it was a mean thing to do."

"What job was that?" Ted asked. He swung around and looked at the marching boys and girls and spotted the fellow he was looking for. "Hey, Dan," he called, "come here."

Dan told Ted to drop dead.

Instead, Ted went to the foot of the pier and yelled: "Halt!" Everyone did halt, some looking surprised, others angry, still others a bit pleased because they had been given a chance to rest.

Ted yelled for everybody to hear: "Dan, what's this job you claim Evalin stole from you? Even if Mrs. Murdock wanted to, she couldn't hire you to work on the boat. You know that, too. You checked with the state employment people in Birch Corners. You're a minor, and that job is considered too dangerous for a minor."

Tom Crowell bellowed: "That's a dirty lie!"

Tom soon wished he had kept his mouth shut. "And you were with Dan when he was told that," Ted yelled to Tom. "You kids want proof? Just check in the employment office there!"

Tom slammed his sign down. "Boy," Tom raged, "what a guy won't do to make points with a summer girl! Look, Ted, you mind your business and we'll mind ours, okay?"

Evalin looked incredulously at Dan Wyatt. For the first time she began to feel genuine anger with him. Childishly, she wanted to scream something that would cut him to the quick, but all she could think of was: "For shame!"

Three things happened fast.

Sue Winthrop darted forward and slapped Ted Pillsbury's face. She begged everyone to listen to her a moment, but no one did. Signs were tossed to the ground and all the kids headed up the street in the general direction of the Strawberry Goo. And then, excitedly, Sue left, too, not nearly so cocky now as she had been just a few minutes before.

Dumbfounded by the swift turn of events, Evalin went back to her grandmother's yard and sat down shakily under the apple tree. Ted joined her there, his eyes twinkling, his big white teeth gleaming merrily. "Now there's a switch," Ted said, "isn't it? I'm supposed to be in Sue's pocket, yet I side with you."

For some reason, Evalin suddenly felt deeply scared. Almost in a panic, she asked Ted: "What's going on? Ted, I don't know Princess Town this year! Everyone is so different; everyone seems to have a chip on his shoulder. What's going on?"

"Unlax, Mouse."

"Will you not call me mouse, please? I hate that nickname. I don't know why Grammy calls me that."

"If I tell you what's going on, you won't like it."

Evalin almost withdrew the question. Looking around through the deepening twilight, she suddenly decided she did not want the mystery explained. She grew afraid that the answer to the mystery would in some way change her attitude toward the kids of the town and even destroy the love she had always had for Princess Town. And yet some cross-grain in her character prevented her from withdrawing the question.

"Well," Ted said candidly, "we're all growing

up. Let's face it, Evalin: we're none of us dumb bunnies anymore. So think a minute about the local boys and girls. Our folks are just average working people. Only a few of us will ever get to college, and probably none of us will ever live in the style you summer people live in. Well, some of the kids are bound to resent that, especially when they see the way some of you summer people throw your money and weight around. Call it envy. Sure, that's what it is. So that explains the chip on their shoulders."

"But none of that's our fault!"

"Maybe not. But that explains why it was so easy for Sue to talk the kids into picketing the ferryboat. And here's something else you don't know. Most of you summer people care only about yourselves. You come down here just for fun, and you don't care how many kids you hurt or use to have your fun. Not you yourself, actually. All in all, you're friendly and considerate except when you decide you're a reigning beauty."

"I never decide that!"

Ted's laugh made Evalin blush.

"Well," she modified, "I hardly ever decide that. And I haven't once decided that this summer. You check up and see. Glory, I've been too busy."

"Anyway, that's the mystery you wanted explained. The girls want clothes as expensive as yours, but can't have them. Everybody wants a good education, but not everybody will have one. Everybody wants to be treated as equals, as they used to be treated. But to Sue and a lot of others, they're just peasants. Catch?"

Mr. Pike came along, singing, "Blow the Man Down," in a rather pleasant bass voice. He did not notice them under the apple tree, and Evalin almost let him go on to Murdock House alone. But if she did that, she thought, she would probably have to sit there for hours with Ted talking about unpleasant things. And she had had enough unpleasantness on this Saturday, this day off, this day that was supposed to have been hers to enjoy. Suddenly she wanted to end the day, to close her eyes to the world and its people and unpleasantness. She said quickly, before Ted could stop her:

"Hi, there, Mr. Pike; wait for me."

Mr. Pike halted in midstride. But he was a man, darn it, and all males apparently stuck together. "Well, there, Ted," he called genially, "nice to see you. Come on in and have some cocoa and angel food cake. Oh, and don't mind the glares of this young lady. Sam Pike is taking over around here. Come on in and see."

So they all went into the living room. Grammy protested when Mr. Pike said she had gloated quite long enough over the week's receipts. Her protests were ignored. Mr. Pike put the receipt book away and turned on a couple of lamps and waved Ted to a chair near the fireplace. He made Evalin go to the kitchen with him, and together they made cocoa and served refreshments.

"A nice way to end the day," Mr. Pike commented. "Mrs. Murdock, I begin to feel quite like a family man. Does the head of the family give orders? Sure. Well, tomorrow you go for a long drive with Ted. That's why he's here: to invite you. Accept, please."

"Now see here, Sam—"

Then, glory be, Grammy actually blushed and said she would be happy to go riding with Ted tomorrow!

Evalin giggled.

Such a day, she thought, such a day!

Chapter 9

Around the middle of the week, Mr. Pike gave more orders. He came aboard the *Sea Hawk* while Evalin was swabbing down the decks preparatory to the late-afternoon and evening trips across the Princess River. Mr. Pike turned off the hose. "Change into something clean and pretty," he ordered. "I want you to spend some time at the Strawberry Goo. Who knows? Perhaps the kids are sorry. Perhaps if you show your face in town, they'll even tell you so."

Caught by surprise, Evalin looked speechlessly first at him and then down at her bare, wet feet. Finally she went to the house to dress. Up in her cute second-floor bedroom, she put on rust-colored slacks. With the slacks, Evalin wore a short-sleeved tan cashmere sweater and matching denim-topped, crepe-soled flats. She tried her hair up but disliked it that way, and she tried lipstick but thought it too dressy. In the end, she took just plain old unadorned Evalin Mitchell herself into town and ambled hopefully into the Strawberry Goo across the road from the post office. Mrs. Carstairs behind the serving counter made things a bit easier for her by crying out in a jolly way, "Well, look who's finally decided to pay me a visit! Hi, Evalin, long time no see. Have a Goo on the house. You're too thin, girl! Why, you wouldn't weigh ninety pounds dripping wet!"

All the chatter of the boys and girls stopped. All eyes swung in Evalin's direction. For a moment Evalin felt so nervous that her stomach muscles quivered. Her instincts told her that this was a critical moment, but just the same she almost turned to flee from those stares and solemn faces. Just in time, however, she remembered her father's cure for rising panic. To herself Evalin said fiercely: "Gleek!" It worked again. Although she remained a bit nervous, she did stop feeling afraid enough to flee!

Sandra Buell surprised her. At the end of the long, narrow room, Sandra stood up and called, "Park here, honey. Doris and I are hating boys this week, and we're pretty darned lonesome."

At once, all the boys in the place began to tease Sandra and Doris. When Evalin joined the girls in the end booth, a grinning, freckled Mike Tilburn declared, "I never could stand pretty girls. See what snobs they are!"

Everyone laughed.

Mike put some change into the juke box and came to the end booth and sank mockingly to his knees before Doris. "One dance, please?" Mike implored. "Look, I did *not* laugh at you on the picket line. I laughed *with* you."

Doris waved her hand disdainfully. It was a most regal gesture, and her voice matched it. "Scoot, boy, scoot," Doris said in bored tones. "My, you boys are almost as bad as the mosquitoes this year!"

Everyone laughed when Mike got hold of another fellow and the two idiots began to dance a waltz. Presently everyone except the three girls was dancing, and it seemed like old times in the big, gaily decorated hangout. Although Mrs. Carstairs did not allow Evalin to pay for her Goo, she did accept a dollar from Evalin for a Goo apiece for Sandra and Doris. The three girls clashed spoons together over the confections as they always did before they ate. Doris said, "Cheers." Sandra winked.

Then there was interesting talk.

"Hear and weep," Sandra said. "You have two major enemies still: Sue Winthrop and Tom Crowell. I don't think either of them will ever forgive you for their mortification near the pier that evening. The worst thing in the world, in my opinion, is being exposed as a conniving liar before people who trusted you."

"Now the freeze is on them," Doris elaborated. "There's a funny switch. But if you don't think it's serious, hear this: Mike Tilburn actually turned down some work Sue offered to pay him for."

"That was silly," Evalin commented.

Sandra arched her bushy brows. "How come you think so? Personally, I think people ought to fight for principles."

"Sure. I'm all for principles myself," Evalin explained seriously. "But it seems to me that Mike isn't thinking very logically. It seems to me, actually, that he's bringing together two issues that ought to be kept separate. For instance, what has working for Sue got to do with the difference between her principles and his?"

"Would you work for her if you were Mike?" Sandra asked.

"Yup."

"Why?"

"Well, you have to take work where you can get it, don't you? Glory, if you asked every person you worked for what his principles are—"

Evalin broke off. Mike was back again to clown around some more. This time, Mike was asking *her* to dance with him.

Evalin felt tempted.

Golly, did she feel tempted!

Why, she had not had a good dance since her summer in Princess Town had begun!

Still?

"All for one and one for all," she told Mike coldly. "That's how we three are."

Mike ordered: "Slide over for heap big talk, and pronto."

Amused, Evalin did.

Mike sat down and rested his forearms on the table and asked Doris outright, "Are you joking or are you serious? If you're serious against Mike Tilburn, you're nuts."

"It so happens that I was in agony that evening. It was a blister."

"How did I know that? I thought you were just making like a comic to keep morale high."

Doris sniffed.

Evalin, grinning, decided that the sniff was just an act. But Doris had to be given an out to save her pride, of course. So?

"Guess what?" she asked Doris.

Doris asked: "What?"

"Even Sue Winthrop thought you were putting on an act. You certainly fooled everyone."

"Really?"

"Even I thought you were putting on an act. It's hard to tell about you. Remember that play you kids put on a couple of years ago during Yacht Club Day? You screeched at the king in the play, and you certainly convinced me you hated the king."

Doris was thrilled. Quite happily and excitedly she said, "I could always act. My mother thinks that if I had some training I could be a professional actress."

And at once Doris graciously forgave poor Mike. "All right, ninny," Doris said, "let's twirl."

Surprisingly, Mike said, "In a couple of minutes. Heap big talk first. Look, Evalin, you might as well know most of the gang is sorry, and you won't have trouble with them any more. But Sue Winthrop is a lousy loser. So she's going to give you trouble. What she has in mind is asking the state employment people how come you, a minor, can work on the ferryboat if the other kids can't. See?"

It jolted Evalin.

Mike surprised her a second time. "Another thing, Evalin, is this. It so happens that the day before yesterday I did some work for Dr. McGrath. He asked me to pass a message to the gang that you're the only person he knows who can keep Mrs. Murdock from going broke while she's in that wheel chair. Brother! Why were you too high and mighty proud to clue us in about the money situation? If there's one thing most of us kids around here understand, it's a tight money situation."

Evalin had to look down at her almost finished Goo.

Sandra wagged her head. "Adults are strange," Sandra commented to no one in particular. "They tell us that pride goeth before a fall. But who puts on a proud smile here? An adult!"

Doris proposed: "Let's all go scratch out the

eyes of a Winthrop, shall we? And as for *you*, Evalin Mitchell, you deserved all the booing you were given! Imagine keeping a secret like that from Sandra and me! What are friends for! To tell your troubles to, that's what!"

"Well, you can't go around discussing someone's personal business," Evalin defended herself. "You just can't do such things!"

Doris chuckled and rose. "It pleases me to dance," she said to Mike quite haughtily. "Shall we or shall we not twirl?"

The next hour was the happiest Evalin had known in weeks. Mike danced with her, too, and once he had gotten her onto the floor just about every boy in the place cut in. Nor did anyone refer to the unpleasantness that had ended. It was quite as if nothing had happened to impair their good relations. Somehow everyone managed to make Evalin feel she was one of the gang again. It was a grand feeling. Laughing, liking everyone, Evalin suddenly decided that they were grand boys and girls after all.

When she returned to Murdock House she surprised both Mr. Pike and herself by kissing him on the cheek saying, "Gramps, everything is under control!"

Chapter 10

On Yacht Club Day, however, Evalin discovered to her sorrow that not quite everything was under control. Like practically all the kids in town, she was early on July the fifteenth to the big boat basin on the north edge of Town Creek. All the summer boys and girls were quite excited. They chattered about the races scheduled for the afternoon, and they chattered about the costume ball scheduled for that evening. The girls busily honey-talked the handsomest boys first and then went down the line to even the homeliest boys to make sure of a partner for every dance. The boys, naturally, played hard to get, and some of them were actually opportunistic enough to make deals for other entertainments before they would agree to sign their names to dance cards. One boy, Greg Lindquist, was a particularly hard bargainer. Just after MaryAnn had asked Greg to be her square-dance partner, Greg said he would certainly enjoy an afternoon picnic at the Bishop place on Heron Creek. And then he had the colossal nerve to stipulate the sort of food he expected MaryAnn to provide. "Smoked turkey," Greg said. "Iced crab, too. And don't forget the ginger ale, either. Not too cold, though."

Evalin interrupted to say that in her opinion MaryAnn would be silly to make such a deal. "Look at yourself in a mirror!" Evalin ordered MaryAnn. "Why, you'll be the belle of the ball! What you ought to do is make the boys pay *you* for a dance!"

"That'll be the day," Greg said scornfully. "The only reason I go to the silly dance is that my folks insist. I'd rather go fishing any old night of the week."

To Evalin's disgust, MaryAnn accepted the deal Greg had outlined. Nor was MaryAnn at all ashamed of herself. "Nine down, two to go!" MaryAnn cried with satisfaction. "What about Ted Pillsbury? You get me a dance with him and I'll get you one with Dirk Jensen. Do you know Dirk? His father does something very elegant in Washington, D.C. Dirk saw you in your ferry-boat rags one day, and he hasn't been the same boy since."

Evalin sighed and looked wistfully toward the big, white-frame Yacht Club building. "Actually," she confessed, "I'm not attending the dance. First of all, none of the town boys has been invited. And secondly, I'm still on probation, you know."

"Ridiculous!"

Evalin deliberately chose to seem to misunderstand. "Sure it's ridiculous," she agreed. "The town boys are certainly as nice as the summer boys, even if they aren't as rich. Personally, I think it's darned undemocratic of the Yacht Club governors to say only the summer kids are good enough to be invited to the ball."

There was an ugly-sounding laugh behind

them. Evalin turned, a bit annoyed, and found the cat-green eyes of Sue Winthrop taking her measure. Lovely Sue just stood there, hands on her hips, her figure beautifully set off by her white shorts and blue-striped T-shirt.

"Shall we have a revolution?" She asked mockingly. "Shall we invite even the farmer boys to come from their smelly old barns?"

Determined not to become involved in any more unpleasantness, Evalin tried to go on with MaryAnn along the catwalks leading to the Bishop cruiser.

She would not have it that way, though. "I find it peculiar," Sue went on, "that you were invited, Evalin. Look at your hands! Why, they're the hands of a peasant! I really don't understand why the governors invited you."

MaryAnn Bishop, it developed, was not a girl to stand by idly while a friend was being insulted. Her black eyes flashing, MaryAnn marched straight up to Miss Susan Winthrop and declared: "I'd rather have a dozen of her at the ball than one of you. Talk about a pathetic, unscrupulous character! You did your best with your fibs to hurt Mrs. Murdock, and you're still doing your best to hurt her. What are you trying to do: drive Evalin away from the Eastern Shore so that you can have all the boys to yourself?"

"At least I'm not a traitor to my class!"

MaryAnn said: "Three cheers for our glorious class! Only where I come from it's considered rude to invite some people to a dance and not others."

"Why bother to attend, then?"

With a snort, MaryAnn swung away from Sue. But Sue had given her something to think about. MaryAnn looked at Evalin in a queer way, and then she asked: "Are you really skipping the dance for the reason you gave or are you doing so to express your opinion of the rudeness?"

Evalin shrugged, not wanting to say anything that would incline MaryAnn to do something impulsive.

MaryAnn acted anyway. Suddenly she gave her head a toss and ripped her dance card into bits. "Count me out, too," she told Sue Winthrop. "I think I'll have a dance this evening at my own place. Only the so-called peasants are invited, so please stay here, there's a sweet."

Sue proved that she had a very quick mind. "So that's what you're up to!" she said to Evalin. "You want to spoil our fun. You aren't having any fun, so you don't want others to. You know perfectly well that girls can invite the local kids to the dance if we want to. We're just trying to keep the herd out."

The words were wasted, however. MaryAnn linked arms with Evalin and drew her along the catwalk to the big Bishop cruiser. Once they were aboard, MaryAnn tooted the whistle a couple of times to attract the attention of the Princess Town boys and girls lining the shore. MaryAnn made a cute little speech, yelling herself red in the face as she did so.

"Now hear this!" MaryAnn yelled. "Evalin Mitchell and I are giving a dance at the Bishop place tonight for the Princess Town guys and gals only! Come as you are! Come prepared to dance and eat! Free transportation aboard the *Sea Hawk* at six o'clock! Step right up, ladies and gentlemen, and have a ball!"

The cheers were deafening!

And then a comical thing occurred. Summer boys and girls came running toward the cruiser, demanding that they be allowed to attend, too. Greg actually said he would dance twice with MaryAnn free of charge if she would just let him come. MaryAnn waved him away quite regally. "Woo Sue," she said. "Hurrah for the lower classes!"

Then and there, Evalin abandoned her plans to remain at the Yacht Club to watch the races. Quite excited, hugely pleased with MaryAnn, Evalin loped back home to give Grammy the big news.

Grammy was sitting in her wheel chair on the ferryboat pier, Mr. Pike with her. Mr. Pike had brought field glasses along so that Grammy and he could identify the crews of the various boats that would participate in the races. Also, Mr. Pike had brought along a colorful beach umbrella to shade Grammy from the glaring sun. The two were bickering pleasantly about the umbrella when Evalin reached them. Grammy, it seemed, considered it sissy to use the umbrella. "Girl and woman," she was telling Mr. Pike, "I've been bearing up under this Eastern Shore sun for more years than I care to remember. Sun is good for you. Actually, there's nothing wrong with me that getting out of this wheel chair won't cure."

Mr. Pike looked pleadingly at Evalin. Evalin had her own fish to fry, though, and so she refused to risk angering Grammy just to please him.

Grammy noticed the excitement in Evalin's eyes. "Mouse," she said, "if you don't let that excitement out of your system, you'll burst. Tell Grammy."

"MaryAnn and I have decided to give a dance at her place tonight for the Princess Town kids. Grammy, they weren't invited to the costume ball! How mean!"

Mr. Pike made a peculiar grunting sound.

It was practical Grammy who got to the heart of the matter, though. "Something tells me," Grammy said, "that you want me to sail the kids to Heron Creek aboard the *Sea Hawk*."

"Couldn't we, Grammy? I'd gladly pay for the fuel."

"Would you, now! Mr. Pike, see the rich young lady I'm related to!"

But Grammy was smiling. Definitely, the *Sea Hawk* would sail at six o'clock!

Mr. Pike asked: "Can the ferryboat get into Heron Creek, Mrs. Murdock? I didn't know that. And how do you dock?"

"I don't know."

Evalin swallowed hard. Glory smoke, she thought, MaryAnn and she had been to darned hasty!

Suddenly Grammy gave a chuckle. Her eyes lighted up with her old love of adventure. "But we'll pretty quick find out!" she told Mr. Pike. "Everybody aboard! What a grand day for adventuring!"

Nor was argument permitted by the mere man who always said he was taking over. Grammy wheeled herself up the gangplank and got the motor throbbing in jig time. Evalin undid the mooring lines and hopped aboard with a sure-footed grace that caused Grammy to nod. "Oh, you're becoming a sailor," Grammy said. "It's your Murdock blood, of course. The Murdocks have salt in their blood, all right."

As if to brag about all the salt in the blood of the Murdocks, Grammy tooted the whistle five times and then revved the motor up to thunder. The fat ferryboat plowed ahead, kicking up a spray that gleamed prettily between sky and river. Up in the bow, even Mr. Pike became silly, as if infected by Grammy's high spirits. Mr. Pike began to sing: "Blow the Man Down, Bullies," in as booming a bass voice as ever rose from the deck of a boat. Evalin went up front and joined him in the choruses, thinking that if every day could be like this one Grammy would be her healthy self in no time at all.

Grammy kept the ferryboat pounding ahead at three-quarter speed until they neared Heron Creek. Then, by golly, if a certain red-haired girl on a certain islet in the mouth of the creek did not wave to Evalin for help once more! Evalin could hardly believe her eyes. Why in the world, she wondered, was Jamie Holloway always being practically marooned there?

Grammy halted the ferryboat about a hundred yards from the creek. Jamie kept gesturing for them to come closer, but Grammy refused. "Jamie," Grammy yelled, "you know how to swim! Anyhow, a bath will do you good!"

In the end, Jamie swam to them. Evalin lowered a line, and Jamie used the line to scramble up to the low, square-ended stern deck. "Wet," Jamie said. "You know about jellyfish?"

Evalin nodded.

"My, but they sting you over there!" Jamie pointed to her left shin. It was almost ringed by a pink stripe that was darkening with each passing second. Jamie shook her head and asked if they had any mud aboard. Grammy yelled that lemon juice would take the pain out of the sting, so Evalin led Jamie into the galley. While Jamie sat there dripping water and holding her leg up, Evalin squeezed a lemon onto her skin and then spread the juice around the welt the sting was beginning to raise. Jamie said blissfully, "My, but that feels good! You want to see some baby ducks sometime?"

Evalin got some of her spare clothes from her locker, and a towel, too. "Dry off and change," she ordered. "And don't you smile at me, please, because I remember how rude you were the day I rescued you."

Jamie giggled, quite unashamed of herself. "Saved your life," Jamie said. "Phil was so mad! Phil maroons me to make me behave. Crazy brother! I guess he'd have shot you that day if he could've. Why do you think I jumped overboard? Phil doesn't like folks to rescue me. Phil don't like uppity town kids or summer kids."

Evalin was incredulous. "You mean you think he would have *shot* me that day?"

"How come you ain't uppity?"

"Why should I be?"

"Don't you know about us?"

"What's there to know?"

Jamie stood up and twirled about in a wild but happy way. Jamie shouted in a strangely ecstatic voice, "I could show you lots of things! You want me to show you lots of nature things?"

Golly, Evalin thought, but Jamie Holloway was beautiful when she was happy. Some of the flame from her hair seemed to be in her eyes, too; yes, and in all her lively body!

"Sure you do!" Jamie said fiercely. "You got to be lonesome sometimes. Everybody's got to be. So when you're lonesome like Jamie, you come to Pirate's Cove. All right?"

It made Evalin feel queer. After a while, when she could speak, she asked very gently: "Are you truly lonesome, Jamie? Are you?"

Grammy yelled: "Will a loafing sailor below come topside and lend me a hand? Blast it, we have to experiment!"

Evalin went topside, but not before Jamie answered her question with a nod.

Chapter 11

It turned out that there was a bit of the faker in Grammy, too. Grammy eased the ferryboat into Heron Creek as if she had sailed those waters all her life. Moreover, she was able to anchor the ferryboat only ten feet or so from the Bishop pier. And getting all the kids ashore would be a relatively simple matter, Grammy pointed out. Either the Bishop rowboats could be used or a catwalk could be made by stretching planks from the shore to the boat over some pontoons that could be borrowed from Wiley's Ship Yard. Evalin voted in favor of using rowboats, for she had a sneaking suspicion that some overly excited kid would be sure to fall off the catwalk in the dark. With

Jamie, she waded ashore to await the arrival of MaryAnn in the Bishop cruiser. Jamie was quite skittish once they had reached the rolling lawns. "They've got a dog," Jamie said. "Never come here in winter. That dog don't like folks in winter."

A dog did indeed bark as they neared the Bishop's white brick house. It was just a dachshund, however, and practically a puppy at that. Evalin went straight to it and rolled it onto its back and gave its chest a good scratching. Jamie tried to do the same thing, but was too rough. The dog growled a bit and retreated to the steps of the broad, columned porch. There he sat and barked some more until Mrs. Bishop came outdoors to investigate. Mrs. Bishop laughed and wagged a forefinger with mock sternness. "So I have you to thank for too darned much work on too hot an afternoon, Evalin Mitchell! How dare you girls cook up a party without consulting me?"

Evalin introduced Jamie. Mrs. Bishop said introductions were certainly unnecessary but that she was pleased to see Jamie once again. "And here and now," Mrs. Bishop went on to Jamie, "you're hired to spare my poor aching back. Jack-o-lanterns! My very own child insists we string the darned things all over the place! And an hour after I gave Bessie and Bert the day off!"

They were all planning things in the rear patio when MaryAnn arrived at last with what she insisted was sufficient chow to feed an army for a year. Evalin helped MaryAnn unload, and in the process picked up some interesting news. Every Princess Town boy and girl who had been invited by a summer visitor to attend the Yacht Club Ball had decided to attend their party instead. Also, Sue Winthrop was angry enough to chew glass!

"You know what about Sue?" MaryAnn asked.

"What?"

"I never in my life met a girl with a worse set of values! What a strange girl she is! One week she goes all out to become buddy-buddy with the town kids. And the next week, they're not good enough to be invited to a party! What a corkscrew mind! Ugh!"

The subject interested Evalin. After they had

lugged all the supplies to the house, she asked MaryAnn how well she really knew Sue Winthrop. MaryAnn said not very well and that she would not bother to improve her knowledge, either. Evalin told her about the way Sue had behaved the Sunday afternoon she had asked her for the loan of the wheel chair.

MaryAnn whistled.

"The thing that baffles me," Evalin said, "is that she *did* let me have the chair. It's hard to know what to think about her. Sometimes I actually like her. Other times, though—pht!"

"Well, I can understand her attitude toward you," MaryAnn admitted. "You see feuds like the one between you two all the time. At school they call it a personality clash. There's just something in each of you that rubs the other the wrong way. Also, I guess that if I were a pretty blonde, I'd be worried about a pretty brunette, or vice versa."

Evalin was amused by that last remark. "Well, if prettiness is what bugs her, why isn't she equally annoyed with you?"

MaryAnn chuckled. "I stay on my side of the

river, mostly," she said. "Your biggest foe is always the person who's on the same side of the river as you are."

"I'd just as soon not have a feud with her. Actually, there's no reason for one. I couldn't compete for boys even if I wanted to. And actually, I don't want to. Live and let live, that's my motto this summer."

"Send Ted Pillsbury back to her, then!"

"Special delivery?" Evalin got up, deciding they had wasted too much time. "The funny thing is that I seldom see Ted. It's just been my luck that Sue happened to see us together the few times we've been together."

Mrs. Bishop came into the kitchen to see how they were getting along. Mrs. Bishop looked things over and said she doubted Bessie would rejoice in the mess the two girls had made of the kitchen. Just the same, she agreed with Mary-Ann's contention that a messed-up kitchen was preferable to a starvation party, so she put on an apron, too, to help make the sandwiches Mary-Ann had decided to serve buffet-style throughout the dance. For the next three hours, they worked. Even Jamie came in to help, and Jamie was as fine a hand with a knife as anyone Evalin had ever seen, Molly at home included. It was Jamie who trimmed the various cold cuts and sliced the cheeses and sliced the sandwiches into desired shapes. While she worked Jamie nibbled, and the question arose, inevitably, whether all sanitation practices ought to be adhered to or whether Jamie should be kept on the job, sanitary fingers or not. Evalin stoutly insisted that what the guests did not know would not grieve them, and she finally won the argument. Jamie, grateful, gave her sweet glances from then on almost every time a scrap of roast beef or ham or cheese proved irresistible.

They made two hundred sandwiches. These were covered and then put into the well-house to be kept moist and cool. The ingredients for the punch were lugged out to the well-house, too, and then they went into the great rumpus room to see to the floor and the rearrangement of furniture. It was almost three o'clock before MaryAnn pronounced everything as festive as it ought to be.

By that time, poor Jamie was all atwitter about the party. Finally Evalin got her courage together and asked Mrs. Bishop if Jamie might attend. Mrs. Bishop gave her a long look. "Dear," she asked, "have you tried arguing with her brother lately? I'm willing to have her, but is he willing to let her come?"

MaryAnn surprised both Evalin and Mrs. Bishop by declaring in ringing tones: "One for all, all for one." MaryAnn headed bravely for her cruiser, and the three of them made a fast trip to Pirate's Cove. Once they had reached the ramshackle Holloway pier, though, MaryAnn lost her bravery. She gave Evalin a sickly sort of smile. "I'll wait right here," she said. "You won't mind, will you?"

Jamie, Evalin noticed, looked very scared, her face pinched, her body all huddled together as if she were trying to hide it behind herself. Suddenly, for no reason she could think of, Evalin grew furious with Phil Holloway. In her anger she never stopped once to consider the consequences of impulsive action. She just got up onto the land

and marched to the old house with the swayback roof and gave the front door a good thumping. Nor did she retreat an inch when a tall, gangling, glowering boy came out and ordered her to scoot. Remembering that friendliness was always supposed to win the day, she forced a smile and thrust out her hand and said: "Hi, Phil Holloway. I'm a friend of Jamie's."

It did not work.

"We ain't got no friends," he snapped. "Who asked you here? You want me to get sore? You go away!"

"Whether you like it or not," Evalin said, "I am a friend of Jamie's. I'm giving a party with MaryAnn Bishop, and we want her to attend. We want you, to, if you'll just stop glowering like that. Glory, what a crosspatch!"

His face turned almost purple-red.

Understanding, or thinking she did, Evalin swung around and gazed about the Holloway property. The thing that surprised her about it was the neatness she saw everywhere. Off to the left, down toward the creek, was a quite beautiful garden with not one single wilted flower in sight. The lawn was a beautiful stretch of well-trimmed green. And the shrubs were all trimmed, all rising just so from circles of spaded dark earth!

"Nice place," she said. "By the way, you know my grandmother, Mrs. Murdock. Mrs. Murdock loves Jamie, I guess. There, does that make the invitation any better?"

"They don't like us, none of them. Don't you know what my Pa did? He stole, and they stuck him in jail, and he died there."

Evalin bit her lip.

"You know where Ma is?" Phil Holloway demanded. "County hospital, that's where. You know what they want to do to Jamie and me if they get a chance? They want to stick us in a home. I'll shoot them first!"

Evalin said mechanically, as her father had often said to her: "Hey, slow down!"

"You leave us alone and we'll leave you alone."

"But Jamie *wants* to attend the party."

"No!"

He rushed down to the creek, and Jamie cried

out, but he came back with Jamie anyway, cling-
ing tightly to her wrist. "You wanna be marooned?" Phil was yelling. "You stay away from
people! They're no good. They killed Pa, don't
you understand?"

For Evalin, that was quite enough. Her eyes
flashing, all of her feelings outraged, she wound
up and gave Phil Holloway a slap that made her
hand tingle. "For shame!" she told him. "No one
killed your father, and you have no right to say
so or to treat Jamie like that. The trouble with
you is you're antisocial! Maybe if you gave people a chance to know you, they'd surprise you."

Phil Holloway said huskily: "Get off Holloway land. Don't never come back here no more."

Jamie, crying, begged Evalin to leave, so Evalin left. But the whole episode bothered her. Even
during the exciting party that evening, she could
not get the memory of Phil Holloway's antisocial
face out of her mind. In many ways, his face reminded her of the faces of the dreadfully down-
and-out adult men that were sometimes brought
to the university's hospital for special treatment

and even surgery. Once she had asked her father why those men looked as if someone had actually beaten them. Her father had answered: "They have been beaten, I'm afraid, either by life or by themselves or by both."

But Phil Holloway was much too young to look that beaten, that defeated!

Chapter 12

The party given so impulsively by MaryAnn Bishop and Evalin paid rich dividends to Evalin toward the end of the last week in July. In the state employment office in Birch Corners, a Mr. Earnshaw who had summoned her for a "hearing" gave her hand a warm handshake and said genially: "Oh, I know all about you, young lady. You're the rich girl who stole a job from a kid who needed work. You're the traitor to your class. You're the girl who has offended Miss Sue Winthrop. Tut, tut. How do you like being a working girl, by the way?"

"I love it!"

"Do you, now!"

Evalin took the indicated chair. She supposed

she should have informed this Mr. Earnshaw that technically she was not working for her grandmother but just helping out with small chores. All the town kids had urged her to tell the fib at the strategy meeting at the Strawberry Goo that Sandra had called the afternoon Evalin had received the summons from Mr. Earnshaw. Still, Evalin was just as glad she had not fibbed. Years ago she had tried a whopper, but the thing just had not worked out. At the wrong time she had forgotten the details of the whopper she had told, and so she had been taken into her father's study for a lecture. Such lectures from your own father were no fun. Such a lecture from a total stranger such as Mr. Earnshaw would be ghastly!

Mr. Earnshaw rested his forearms on the desk. He was a short man with a great big chest and a bristly head of graying hair. He had small blue eyes, a big nose and a chin with a cleft. The nicest thing about him was his smile. When he smiled, you tended to forget he could be pretty darned tough with kids who worked at the wrong kind of jobs at the wrong time of year.

"What do you like best about the job?" he asked.

"Sailing. Every trip is different, somehow. This time it's the sky; another time it's the water; another time it's the wind; still another time it's the way the land smells and the river smells get all mixed up."

"You're a born sailor, then. But I'd expect that, you having Murdock blood in your veins. How is your grandmother, by the way?"

Evalin told him happily: "Improving. Her blood pressure is down, and her leg is feeling pretty good. Dr. McGrath told her the other day that he's afraid she'll live to marry Mr. Pike."

"Grand. Now listen to me a moment. The trouble with being the one-man crew of a busy office such as this is that you tend to follow the rule book too closely. You do that because it simplifies your work. But that can be the wrong thing to do, as some boys and girls from Princess Town convinced me a few days ago. You're very lucky, by the way, to have such good friends. Last week I planned to tell you in no uncertain terms to get off the *Sea Hawk* and stay off. Then these youngsters paid me a surprise visit and we had quite a lively discussion. A fellow named Tom Crowell and another fellow named Dan Wyatt claimed that if I would just make an observation trip on the *Sea Hawk,* I'd discover your work isn't at all dangerous."

Evalin asked weakly: "Dan Wyatt?"

"Yup. Well, to make a long story short, I did make an observation trip on Sunday. Obviously, your work isn't at all dangerous, not nearly as dangerous as farm work can be, I'll tell you that. So I checked with my superior in Baltimore, and he told me to use my own judgment. Now get this, please. You definitely must not ever make a trip alone. You're a minor, and a minor must not be given responsibility for the safety of the ferryboat passengers. But as long as Mrs. Murdock or Mr. Pike or some qualified, responsible adult is aboard to supervise, you may work aboard the ferryboat to your heart's content. Any questions?"

Too elated to speak, Evalin shook her head and ran, afraid he might change his mind.

The next dividends from the party came in the form of three beautiful fish. Evalin found them on the back porch one evening when she went outdoors to hang up the dish towel. The fish were so firm and cold to the touch that she knew they could not have been out of the water longer than an hour. Moreover, they had been cleaned so thoroughly she knew they were the gift of an expert fisherman. But who?

Grammy, in the kitchen, put on a greedy expression the moment she saw the fish. "About time!" she said. "I've been getting a real craving for a fish dinner. Catch them from the pier?"

"Found them on the back porch, addressed to me."

"So! And I thought it was understood you'd seek no romantic conquests here!"

Evalin ruffled her gray hair fondly. "Simmer down," she advised. "I'd hardly call three dead fish glorious tokens of eternal love."

The telephone rang in the living room. Evalin answered, being quicker, and was glad she had. A tough, rasping voice asked: "You find them hardhead?"

"Why, Phil Holloway!"

"Don't you bother us, you hear? We don't want nothing from nobody! She's crazy, that Jamie! Why should we give you eating fish? But she kept saying you invited her to that party. What's a crazy party? Who cares about a crazy party? Girls are nuts!"

Moisture came to Evalin's eyes. Managing to keep emotional trembles from her voice, she said: "It's a thoughtful gift, Phil. I've never been given such nice fat fish before. You should have seen Grammy's face when I took those fish into the kitchen. Guess who'll have a fish dinner tomorrow evening?"

Phil broke the connection, but the seeming rudeness did not irk Evalin even a little bit. She reported the conversation to Grammy while she put the fish away in the refrigerator. Grammy listened quite attentively for a change, her bushy brows drawn together, her head cocked over her left shoulder. When Evalin had finished, Grammy gave a shrug that could have meant anything.

Then Grammy said in thoughtful tones, "I used to think, Mouse, that I'd take those Holloway kids under my wing. They've led a rough life. They don't want for food or clothes, because the county welfare people look after them. But what kind of life is that? Phil's a pretty smart fellow, don't think he isn't. And take Jamie. If somebody could keep her in school and give her guidance and even inspiration, Jamie would lead her class. It's a problem."

Evalin sat down on the dinette table, quite curious. "Grammy, how do these things operate? I mean, what really goes on when the county takes a family under its wing?"

"How should I know?"

"I thought you once told me a Murdock knows everything."

Grammy made muttering sounds. Grammy looked most suspiciously at Evalin's face. Evalin contrived to look properly interested and repectful and solemn. After a minute or so, Grammy said, "Actually, I guess the welfare people handle these things the way I handle the *Sea Hawk*. I couldn't give you any hard and fast rules for handling the *Sea Hawk,* could I? Different conditions call for different methods. If the wind is coming dead on and kicking up a heavy sea, I angle to starboard as I leave the pier. But if it's a calm sea I push straight out from the pier. See? Well, that's pretty much how the welfare people have to operate. They have general methods, sure, just as I have. But they fit their specific methods to the specific conditions."

"Why don't they insist Jamie go to school?"

"They do. And Jamie goes for a while. Then she takes off like the wild creature she is. Well, what are the county people going to do? We don't have special schools in this county, and you can't jail a girl because she won't go to school. So they find Jamie and they scold her, and she behaves for a while, and then she takes off again. What does she do? Who knows? We do know, of course, that Jamie behaves pretty well. Don't you ever think otherwise. I know that redhead. She doesn't have a mean or a dishonest bone in her. What it all amounts to, I guess, is that her family problems have given her a philosophy that's different from the average girl's."

Evalin was enchanted. She herself had yet to find a philosophy that meant anything to her. Most of the things she did from day to day were done because they were expected of her. Little if any of her actions and thoughts evolved from a philosophy that had been developed by her own intellect to suit her own particular temperament and aspirations. And that wild redhead had actually developed her own philosophy? Well!

"The trouble is," Grammy went on, "that those kids would be too much for me. They've been on their own too long. Then, of course, there's Mrs. Holloway. You can't just take kids from their mother, you know. When she's home, she looks after them pretty well."

"What's wrong with her, Grammy?"

"Broken heart, mostly, in my opinion. Oh, a lot of physical things, too, I guess. She just went to pieces after Mr. Holloway died in jail. First she got a bad case of shingles. Then she had a nervous breakdown. Then—"

But Grammy never got any further. Just like that, Evalin had an inspiration. "Whoa," Evalin said, her eyes shining. "Grammy, don't you see? Why, it would be perfect! You could help them and they could help you! Glory smoke, I'm a genius!"

Grammy could be very perceptive, her many years considered. "Pish and tush," she said. "I had that same idea weeks ago. Sure, it seems like a good idea, all right. I take them in, and they help me with the ferryboat. Tit for tat and hurrah for all! Only one thing's wrong. What makes you think the kids would come here and settle down to a life of study and work? Take a bird that's been wild and free. You think that bird will be happy in a cage? You think that bird will even come near a cage?"

"But they can't go on as they're going, Grammy. Life will pass them by. Ask Miss Rosen."

"Miss Rosen? Who's she?"

"My counselor at Cantwell High. According to Miss Rosen, people my age will one day live in a world a lot more complex than the world of today.

According to Miss Rosen, people possessed of little education will have a very difficult time earning a bare living. So all the good things in life will pass them by. And that's a terrible thing, Grammy, just terrible."

Grammy shrugged. "Life's that way," she said rather indifferently. "Some people get a lot; others get a little. Anyway, it's no skin off your nose, Mouse. Do you know something? I'm beginning to feel like a darned poor hostess. You came down here for a summer of fun. And all you've had is work, problems, more work, more problems."

"Actually," Evalin told her, "I've never been happier. And that's strange, in a way. Won't Molly be stunned when I tell her about this summer! According to Molly, I'm just a harum-scarum teen-ager they ought to put to sleep and not wake up until I'm thirty years old!"

"Remind me to write Molly a nasty letter."

"Don't you dare!"

Grammy chuckled.

"Anyway," Evalin told her, "it's sort of interesting to meet challenges and solve problems. Dad and Mom always say that, and I'm beginning to see what they mean. I'll tell you one thing, Grammy. I'll never again doubt my ability to do whatever I must do. Why, I can even crawl out of the feathers at five in the morning now, all charged up and raring to go."

A whistle sounded out in the yard. It made Evalin blush, and she came close to pretending she had not heard it. But Grammy said tenderly, "Mouse, as far as I'm concerned, you're off probation for the rest of the summer. Arranging that party for the town kids was a darned kind thing to do. A girl who's that kind isn't going to be too cruel to stupid boys."

"Well, it made MaryAnn and me hopping mad! But you have to be fair, Grammy. It was MaryAnn's idea; not mine."

Grammy said dryly: "Well, I'll allow her to see boys now and again the rest of the summer, too."

Laughing, Evalin went out to the front yard. It was Dan Wyatt, come at last as he always had in other years, a bucket in one hand, a powerful

flashlight in the other. He was not pleased to see
Evalin in a dress and elegant shoes. "I thought
we'd go baiting," Dan said. "How can you go
baiting like that?"

"Ugh."

But Evalin changed, and they went to the river,
and they followed the shoreline awhile until they
came to Kingfisher Point. Dan took off his shoes
and socks and went down to the wet, squishy
sand. Whenever he yelled: "Now!" Evalin turned
the flashlight on, and Dan worked feverishly with
his net to catch the minnows attracted by the light.
It was two hours before Dan had anything worth-
while in his bait pail. But who cared? How nice it
was, Evalin thought, to be bumming around with
Dan again.

Chapter 13

On her next day off, threats notwithstanding, Evalin got the catboat out early and headed up-river to Pirate's Cove. When she got abreast of Town Park, however, she had to beach the boat because Mrs. Riley, the publisher and editor of the *Princess Town Times,* was beckoning to her urgently. Mrs. Riley ordered: "Mitchell, you come with me."

Nor would Mrs. Riley accept the quick polite excuse Evalin gave for wanting to sail on. Evalin had to lower the sail and tie it around the boom and go with Mrs. Riley to her office building on Morris Way. In a sense, it was a pleasant walk. At that hour, they had the lovely summer morning

the shrubs and trees and flowers looked fresh in
the sweet morning air, all the birds were stirring
about and singing. Evalin spotted a dozen Baltimore orioles before they had walked a block.
to themselves. All the sky was salmon pink, all
Also, amusingly, she spotted several squirrels
frisking about playfully in one of the great horse-
chestnut trees. At that hour of the day, Evalin decided, a person saw old Princess Town at its best.

In her office, Mrs. Riley said, "I'm glad I saw
you, Mitchell. I've been hearing all sorts of things
about you."

"Nice things, I hope?"

Smiling, Mrs. Riley waved her to a chair. Mrs.
Riley put on a purple smock and went behind her
big, cluttered desk. A slender woman, Mrs. Riley
was particularly interesting to look at because
every curl and wave of her blonde hair was just so
and the rest of her grooming was equally perfect.
Evalin's personal opinion was that Mrs. Riley
tended to dress too drably, so she was rather
pleased about the smock. The smock and Mrs.
Riley's eyes, she noticed, were almost the same

shade of purple.

"Don't ever publish a newspaper," Mrs. Riley told her, crinkling her nose. "Work, work, work. And some days the writing is difficult, believe me. What do you plan to work at, incidentally?"

"No plans, I'm afraid. Mother wants me to be a nurse, Dad wants me to be a surgeon, Grammy wants me to be a ferryboat captain. Sometimes I think I'd like to be an ornithologist and other times I think I'd like to be in business."

"In other words, you haven't jelled, intellectually speaking? Well, that happens, especially, I imagine, when there's no pressure to earn an income. The reason I asked the question is that Mr. Earnshaw seems to believe you can help me establish a summer project or tradition that needs to be established in Princess Town. What did you think of Mr. Earnshaw?"

"He seemed nice, understanding. Of course, I only talked to him a little while."

"Well, let me tell you something about him. Mr. Earnshaw's work with the state involves the young—the kids looking for their first permanent jobs, other kids looking for summer jobs. Princess Town is a problem because most of the work around here is seasonal, and the good season for finding work happens to be when the boys and girls are in school. Oystering, fishing, crab canning, farming—those are the major industries. Tough on the youngsters, don't you think?"

Evalin nodded, beginning to wonder about this project.

"But there's one possible solution to the problem," Mrs. Riley went on: "the tourist business. Or, more specifically, the people who have summer homes here. It seemed to me, and Mr. Earnshaw agrees, that a campaign to get the summer people to give summer jobs to the youngsters around here might help us solve part of the problem. Well, that's the project I thought you might help me with. Actually, you're the ideal person to help. You're part of the summer crowd, yet you're quite popular with the local crowd. You could explain the need to the summer people, and you could explain the ways of the summer people to the local boys and girls."

"But this is practically August, Mrs. Riley."

"So it is. And probably we could do little more than get the project under way this year. But that would be progress, you see. Next year, the summer people would automatically include in their plans the work one or two school youngsters could do for them. Within a few years, if it were all handled correctly, it would be traditional to reserve certain jobs for our school kids. You see?"

"Probably this will be my last full summer here, though."

"Who knows? But suppose it is. Wouldn't it give you satisfaction to know how you had helped to start something of benefit to all your friends here?"

"Of course!"

Mrs. Riley took a sheaf of papers from the middle drawer of her desk. "Actually," she said, "I've written the first story about the project. It seemed to me that you might agree to lend your name to it, so you'll notice your name here and there. The next story will have to be written by you, however."

Evalin stared and almost laughed. Glory, she thought, Miss Rigney in Cantwell High would collapse if she heard anyone offering Evalin Mitchell, of all people, the opportunity to write anything for publication! Who was always low girl on the Composition totem pole? Miss Evalin Mitchell!

Curious, Evalin read the story. She had to read it three times before she thoroughly understood the project Mrs. Riley had in mind, but after the last reading she became quite excited. "Why, I'd practically be a clearing house for workers!" she exclaimed. "But where do I find them?"

"Quite simple, Mitchell. This is how we've planned it. Mr. Earnshaw will interview all boys and girls who want summer jobs. He will certify them for whatever work they're qualified to do proficiently. He will provide work papers and all the support he can. Then every week the *Times* will publish a short article urging people to employ these youngsters and thus give them the opportunity to acquire the higher education they'll need in the world of tomorrow. In addition, *you'll* do a short article about the types of jobs the kids have been given. You'll name names, you'll give credit where credit is due. And last but not least, you'll talk up the project whenever you're around summer people. In a sense, you'll be a salesman. Catch?"

"I couldn't do all that alone, Mrs. Riley."

"Get some of your friends to help you. I wish you'd give it a try. I could ask others, and I would, if necessary. But you're my first choice. You seem to like everyone and everyone seems to like you. Also, you happen to have a quite resourceful mind and considerable poise, in the event you don't know. Try?"

"Do you know who could really help if you approached her correctly and if you steamed her up? Sue Winthrop."

"Make her your assistant, then."

Evalin swallowed hard. She could well imagine how Sue would behave if she dared to set foot on the Winthrop estate! Talk about a mortal enemy!

In some fashion or other, Evalin never did know how, Mrs. Riley finally got her way. And then, by golly, Mrs. Riley could not get her out of the office fast enough! *Really!*

But it seemed all right to Evalin after she had gotten out on the river once more. Actually, she thought, she would be doing here in Princess Town more or less the same thing her parents were doing in faraway Thailand: helping people to help themselves. Only this would be better, really, because the people she would be helping happened to be her friends. So Dan Wyatt wanted work so he could go to college? Find him a job! And all the others wanted work? Well, find them jobs, too!

When Evalin reached the Holloway place at last, she found Jamie doing laundry and Phil working in the vegetable garden a hundred feet or so beyond the shabby house. Jamie said: "Run!" Evalin ignored the order. Filled with an odd feeling of confidence, Evalin also ignored the glares Phil gave her when he came running to the back yard. "Hi," she said easily. "Does anyone around here want to earn some cash money?"

Phil told Jamie to go back to work. Jamie re-

fused. Phil said that was what came of associating
with girls, but Jamie just laughed and told him
that he ought to be polite. Phil gave a growl and
sat down on the back stoop.

Jamie asked: "What do you want done, honey?
Phil, he can shoot for you or fish for you or farm
for you. You want housework done? I guess I'm
pretty good when I have the mind to be."

"I thought somebody would like to be my guide
whenever I have the time to explore one of the
creeks. I'm not supposed to explore alone, it
would seem."

Were they interested?

You bet!

"How much cash money?" Phil asked.

"What do you charge around here?"

"Two bits an hour."

Evalin was shocked. Why, back in Cantwell,
the least you paid people to do any kind of work
for you was about a dollar and a half an hour!

Obviously misunderstanding Evalin's hesita-
tion, Jamie said with pathetic eagerness: "What
about twenty cents an hour? Phil, I could do it!

Phil, let me do it! A girl likes new clothes, Phil!"

Evalin had to sit down. The definite hunger for new clothes that showed in Jamie's eyes left Evalin with a peculiar sick feeling in her stomach. For perhaps the first time in her life it occurred to her that she was an incredibly lucky person. All her life she had taken such things as nice clothes and a fine house and good food and a generous allowance for granted. Never had she stopped to think for one moment that all these things taken for granted had had to be earned for her. All had been given to her so freely that never once had she thought in terms of the efforts her folks had made to acquire things for her. Poor Jamie and Phil.

Evalin said to Phil huskily: "I'll pay you seventy-five cents an hour, Phil. As for you, Jamie, I have different plans. You're coming to Murdock House every morning to clean the place and things like that. Grammy will hire you, I'm sure."

Phil said huskily: "There ain't that kind of money. What are you trying to do? You get away from here! You're crazy!"

"No, sir. It just so happens I have an allowance my folks call fun money. If I spend five dollars a week on fun, I'll still have enough left over to buy the little things I need. And Grammy can darned well afford to pay Jamie, because I'm not taking any salary from Grammy and the ferryboat business is getting better and better all the time."

Phil jumped up, tall, too thin, a queer expression on his face. "Who wants charity? Don't you think I'm sick of charity?"

Of all things, Jamie began to cry. She crouched on the porch, beautiful wild thing that she was, and cried without covering her face. Quick as a flash, Phil was beside her, an arm around his sister pulling her close. "Will you hush now?" Phil begged. "Firefly, it's all right. Look, I won't punish you no more; I won't maroon you."

"I want to, I want to, I want to!"

The eager cry went straight to Evalin's heart. Impulsively, feeling emotional enough to do some crying, too, Evalin stood up and said firmly, "It's all settled, Phil. You may rant and rave all you wish, but I'm not going to let life pass either you or Jamie by. Call that crazy, if you want, but that's how I feel. Here and now, like Mr. Pike always says, I'm taking over."

She did not permit him to argue, either! While he stood there sputtering, Evalin ambled back to the creek and got back into the boat. Jamie came wet-faced to the water's edge and begged, "Honey, don't be mad. Please don't be mad, okay?"

Evalin gestured for Jamie to hop aboard. Naturally, Phil hopped aboard also, presumably to protect his sister. Evalin then went amidships and rested her back against the mast. "Cap'n Holloway," she joshed, "be a nice boy, will you, and sail us off to adventure. I just love to explore the different creeks!"

"We ain't even got fit drinking water! How crazy can you get?"

It was surrender!

Phil Holloway, by golly, was *smiling*.

Her voice trembling with happiness, Evalin

said: "Look under the thwart, Cap'n Holloway. Food and water for all."

Then, like Jamie, she took off her shoes and socks and dangled her feet in the water as Phil angled the catboat away from the shore.

Chapter 14

Grammy was of two opinions on the subject of Jamie Holloway. "Mouse," she said, "I could kiss you and shake you at one and the same time. You come down from that bed or I'll come up!"

Chuckling, Evalin remained put on the rainy first day of August.

Thumps sounded on the stairs. Aghast, Evalin sat up and yelled: "Grammy, you'll kill yourself!" But the thumps went on, and presently Grammy was in the room, her face flushed, her brown eyes sparkling. "Donder and Blitzen," Grammy exclaimed, "but it's good to be on the old hoofs!"

Evalin said: "For shame, Grammy."

Grammy sat down near the foot of the bed.

Never particularly sentimental, Grammy became quite sentimental for a moment or two. She pulled Evalin to her and kissed the little chin, the freckled nose. "My, what a hulk you're getting to be," Grammy said. "I don't care much about the way Nature works things out. You were much cuter when you were a tyke."

Evalin giggled. "Grammy, did you save any of my baby hair?"

"Yup."

"No!"

"Baby pictures, too."

"Naked as sin, I suppose. Why do adults always take pictures of poor naked babies?"

"It's a silly custom," Grammy conceded. "But you'll do it, too. The objective, I guess, is to have one picture of the creature as is, before she gets all those silly clothes and silly hairdoes and such. But don't sweet-talk me, young lady! Who's captain of this ship, you or me?"

"You."

"Then why didn't you consult me about Jamie before you hired her?"

"Because you procrastinate."

"Because I what?"

"According to one of our social study teachers in Cantwell, procrastination is a bad habit too many people acquire. I'll prove you procrastinate, too. You told me you wanted to do something for the Holloway kids. But you never got around to doing anything. And all that time poor Jamie was hungry for nice clothes and Phil was sick of charity. Well, if I've learned anything this summer, it's this: action is a lot better than words. Suppose I'd just talked about helping you on the boat? No, ma'am! If it's your duty to do something, then go ahead and do it. Don't put it off until tomorrow or the next day. Tomorrow may never come."

"And what happens, pray tell, when you leave in September?"

"Jamie helps you around the house and Phil helps you on the boat. Grammy, what could be better for everybody concerned?"

"But I won't *need* help on the boat!"

"If you can support me in exchange for work, Grammy, you can support them. Anyway, when you marry Mr. Pike money won't be a screaming problem any more. I've already given my folks that flash."

"So I'm to marry him, eh? How nice of you to decide that for me!"

The telephone rang. Knowing this was the day the Work for School Youngsters project was being announced in the *Princess Town Times,* Evalin rushed downstairs in just her shortie nightgown. To her astonshiment, it was Sue Winthrop, of all people in the world. In quite imperious tones, Sue ordered: "Come running here, please. Don't bother about breakfast; I'll feed you."

Evalin almost snapped sarcastically: "How dear of you!" But at the back of her mind was the restraining thought she was now in the position of being unable to afford offending anyone. Now that she had accepted the responsibility of helping Mrs. Riley and Mr. Earnshaw to get the project going, it would be both childish and wrong to offend anyone as influential as a Winthrop.

"Well?" Sue demanded sharply.

"Do I gild the lily, or what? Technically, I'm

supposed to be a slavey today."

"You know my mother."

Evalin sighed, but when she went upstairs she got the pink outfit from her wardrobe closet and dutifully showered and primped. In the kitchen, where she found Jamie happily chomping away on a huge breakfast of eggs and bacon and fried potatoes and pancakes, she arranged with her grandmother to have the entire morning off. Grammy looked up from the advance copy of the *Times* that Mr. Pike had brought along when he had popped in for a late snack the evening before. "I don't know whether I like living with a dynamo," Grammy said. "No wonder your folks palm you off on me every summer!"

Grinning, Evalin hustled off for talk and breakfast with the Winthrops.

Mrs. Winthrop was quite pleased with the pink coordinates. "I do love girls who dress as girls," Mrs. Winthrop declared. "What a cute effect that lace has! Sue, I do wish you would try pink."

A servant announced that breakfast was waiting, and they went into the many-windowed dining room. Mr. Winthrop was there, looking over the hot dishes placed on the sideboard. He gave Evalin a nod and a big friendly smile. "Not a scrap of poison in any of these dishes," he told her. "But why this war between you and Sue? Silly, if you ask me."

There were so many hot dishes Evalin had difficulty making a selection. She finally took scrambled eggs, and over these she spread mushrooms in thick brown gravy. Ham, of course. Bacon, too. And, naturally, the dollar pancakes that were a tradition in the Winthrop house.

Mr. Winthrop returned to his peace talk after they had gotten the sharp edge off their appetites. A roly-poly man in a gaudy sport shirt, he pointed a finger at Sue and said: "You, first. What's the big argument you have with Evalin?"

To Evalin's relief, Mrs. Winthrop intervened to say, "John, that isn't the way to handle these things. Let the girls thresh the matter out privately after breakfast. If they need our help, we'll help. In the meantime, let's discuss this project Evalin has become involved in. Evalin Mitchell, I begin to suspect you're doomed to become a social worker! Well, good for you! Society can use people who are not too busy to concern themselves with the problems of less lucky people. How does the thing work, please?"

Evalin explained, more or less using the same explanation Mrs. Riley had given her. Mr. Winthrop was particularly interested when Evalin told him that actually the entire project was being supervised by Mr. Earnshaw in Birch Corners. "Now that's great," Mr. Winthrop said. "To be frank, I thought this was just another idea of people who hadn't given the matter the careful thought it deserves. Good work guaranteed, eh?"

"Well, the kids will certainly be qualified to do whatever they're sent to do. Mr. Earnshaw asks them a lot of questions about experience, knowledge, and all that. Say you want a boat painted. If there's a boy who's experienced at that, he's the boy they'll send."

"Personally," Sue said, looking directly at Evalin, "I think that what the project needs is a good manager. Daddy, you know what I mean. You pay

Mr. Quigley a lot of money to manage your workers up north. Why? Because managing is important, isn't that why?"

"Yes. But why do you think they haven't a good
manager? Here's Evalin, and she's already given
me the answers to the questions I wanted to ask."

Sue asked crisply: "Will you check their work,
Evalin? Say I want to hire a boy to pretty up my
miniature golf course. Do you come when he's
finished and check everything before I pay him?"

Mrs. Winthrop said, puzzled: "But you'd not
pay, would you, if you were dissatisfied?"

"Mother, that's my very point! You know very
well that we often pay when we're dissatisfied.
Take the last time you hired a boy to tidy up the
plantings along the south fence. You said after-
ward that you could have done a better job in half
the time without even trying very hard."

"Well, that was different, dear. I knew that the
boy needed a few dollars, and my objective was to
give him the money without embarrassing him."

"Then that was charity!" Sue said fiercely. "It
wasn't a business deal. So there you are! Take this

project. If it's just a way of asking for charity for boys and girls who need money, it won't work very long."

Evalin's respect for Sue went up a notch. That was a darned good point Sue had raised!

"It's a business proposition," Evalin told Sue. "Naturally, the project would die in a week or two if people weren't given value for their money."

Sue leaned forward earnestly. "Then you have to have a manager, someone who is always free to inspect the work before anybody is paid. That stands to reason. Take right now. It so happens that I want someone to rearrange my golf course. I'm tired of playing the same old holes in the same order. I could beat par with my eyes closed, I've played that course so often. All right then, Miss Evalin Mitchell. Do you guarantee good work, complete satisfaction? If so, I'll hire a boy this morning."

Evalin said promptly, taking a huge gamble: "Satisfaction guaranteed."

"I want to use the course tomorrow afternoon at five o'clock. Will you inspect it then, please?"

"Yup."

Sue asked smilingly, "But how can you if you're on the ferryboat, Evalin? And say a dozen jobs were completed tomorrow. When could you inspect all those jobs?"

At the head of the table, Mr. Winthrop began to chuckle. He gave Evalin a merry glance. "Watch out," he warned. "You're being trapped."

Beginning to understand what was in Sue's mind, Evalin took her time about answering Sue's questions. In several ways, Sue had the edge on her, she knew. For example, she could never have invited Sue to breakfast as Sue had invited her if she had done her level best to hurt Sue as Sue had tried to hurt her. She would have been too embarrassed, for one thing. Also, she would have been too fearful of a blistering scolding.

"You don't answer," Sue told her, "because you have no anwer. Really, I don't see why Mrs. Riley didn't come to me first. I could have given my full time to the project."

Mrs. Winthrop said, "Watch it, dear. Your bad taste is showing."

Sue's eyes narrowed.

To prevent a family spat, Evalin said quickly, "I just do the work Mrs. Riley assigns me, Sue. Oh, I guess she would listen to me if I asked her to make you my field manager. The only trouble is that most of the Princess Town boys and girls dislike you."

Mr. Winthrop asked: "Why so?"

Blushing, Sue told him: "I goofed, Dad. It didn't matter to me if they were all invited to the costume ball. But Evalin and MaryAnn sided with them, so I put in my two cents' worth. If anyone happens to be interested, I've been sorry ever since. Darn it, I'm not that snobbish or mean, Evalin Mitchell, and you know it!"

At that point, Evalin forgot the presence of Mr. and Mrs. Winthrop. She asked, genuinely interested, "How come I rub you the wrong way, Sue? I've never intended to. Actually, I've always liked you. Not when you've been mean, of course, but—"

"I like to be first! Is that such a crime?"

Evalin was appalled. "But that's kid stuff!

Don't they teach you anything at your school? You're supposed to be a part of your group. Sure, anyone wants to excel, and more power to you. But it's just plain impossible to be first in everything."

"Well, you certainly appear to be doing all right!"

"Oh, sure. Do you know what I was all last year? A very poor B student. Why have I been on probation this summer? Because, glory, was I a scatty soph!"

Sue actually gasped, "Why," Sue said finally, "I get straight A's without half trying!"

Evalin shrugged. "So there you are. Now who happens to be first?"

"Why, you poor dumb bunny," Sue said, "don't you know how to study? Well, for goodness' sakes, let me show you how!"

After that, the breakfast and the morning became quite pleasant.

Chapter 15

Much to Evalin's satisfaction, Dan Wyatt was the first of the boys to find steady work through the project. One afternoon Evalin received a telephone call from a man who sounded as if he were talking with his mouth filled with mush. He told her that he had a small farm and too darned much stock to handle and that if she had a school kid who would be dependable, he would like to discuss a permanent job with him. Jamie was out at the time, but not Phil. Evalin got on the ferryboat, and then she took a big chance and telephoned Sue she needed transportation and some moral support. Ten minutes later they were driving to the farm, if you please, in the Winthrops' chauffeured limousine. The farm turned out to be a very small but pretty place. The man turned out to be quite old. He talked queerly because he had no upper front teeth. But he knew what he wanted, all right, and for a time it appeared he doubted he could get what he wanted from girls who came to interview prospective employers in a Rolls Royce limousine. "Dog my cats!" he yelled, "what do elegant kids like you know about work?"

Sue started to give him the "my dear man" treatment. Evalin silenced Sue with a glance. She got out of the car and showed the man her red, rather rough hands. He grinned, if a person could be said to be able to grin without grinning teeth. "Dog my cats," he said, "don't you watch them TV commercials? They got stuff to keep a girl's hands unred and smooth."

What the man wanted, it developed, was a strong, dependable boy to work eight hours a day on the farm the rest of the summer and then three hours each afternoon until next summer. If he could find the right boy, he said, he would pay him a dollar an hour and give him vegetables and meat and fruit in season to take home to his folks.

"But he's gotta be good," the man insisted. "If he ain't any good, I'll personally run him off my place. Did you mean what it said in the paper—satisfaction guaranteed?"

"Yes, sir."

"Okay. Girl, send me a boy pretty quick!"

It was Sue who suggested Dan Wyatt. Riding back to town, Sue was all business, and Sue was also good sense. "According to my father," Sue said, "beginnings are crucially important. Well, isn't this a beginning? If Mr. Adams is pleased, others will hear about it. Maybe other farmers will find work for other boys."

"Sounds logical to me. But—"

"The only boy I ever found to do good work every time happens to be Dan Wyatt. I suggest Dan."

"The kids will accuse me of favoritism. They know Dan's always been a special friend."

"Business is business. Poof! In business, you do what you think is the smartest thing and let the critics go bite their own ankles. Ask Daddy."

Somewhat against her better judgment, Evalin telephoned Mr. Earnshaw about the job and recommended that Dan be sent to Mr. Adams. The next day, Dan was at work. That evening, when Evalin again drove out with Sue to check up on the quality of the work, she found Mr. Adams sitting blissfully on his porch, very much content with his new hired hand. "Girl," he said, "I've got some good side meat you can take home with you. I sure like Dan. That boy don't have to be told what to do, and he don't have to be watched, neither. You know a girl that needs work? Okay. Every week I want a real lively girl to come give my place a cleaning. An old fellow like me can sure make a mess in a kitchen."

Again, it was Sue who named the worker to send. "Dolly Enroe," Sue said in the car. "Do you know her? A disgusting tub, really. I mean, is she ever plump! But you ask Cynthia Marlowe about her, and you'll discover Dolly is just the person. Cynthia sometimes hires Dolly on the sly when Mrs. Marlowe has laid down the law."

Again, Mr. Adams was pleased with the re-

sults. What was more, he telephoned Mrs. Riley
at the *Times* office and told her so. His praise of
both his workers and the project naturally caused
a stir not only in Princess Town but in Birch Corners, too. The very next day Evalin received
twenty-eight calls from adults who wanted girls
and boys for such chores as cleaning windows,
painting fences, baby-sitting, and the like. Also,
several business people offered permanent part-
time jobs provided qualified kids could be found.

That evening, Mr. Pike once again "took over."
After Evalin had made the last trip of the day
with Grammy, Mr. Pike came aboard the *Sea
Hawk* and told her the time had come for a long
talk. Evalin joined him on the top of the life-
preserver bin, his favorite perch. A mosquito bothered her for a few seconds, but her flapping hand
finally scared the mosquito into full retreat. They
sat watching the water for a while; it was blue-
green this evening, with the reflections of the
shore trees in its depths. "Pretty," Mr. Pike said.
"I never tire of looking at the water. Do you?"

"Never. I always miss the river when I'm in

Cantwell. But not all rivers are so clear, apparently. Daddy wrote last week that the Menam River in Thailand is pretty muddy. He says the Mekong River, where Chiengmai is, can be clear sometimes, though."

"Tell him about the project?"

"You bet!" Evalin laughed. "As a matter of fact, I was so proud of the honor I sent him a cablegram the day after my talk with Mrs. Riley. Do you know what Daddy wrote? He said that I'm very lucky, because early in my life I've found the key of gold. What on earth is the key of gold? Talk about a deep mystery!"

Mr. Pike asked as a teacher might ask: "Well, what does a key do?"

"Unlocks things, of course."

"Well, what does your father do in Thailand? I mean, what's the general effect of his work? He makes people happier than they were before he operated on them, doesn't he?"

"I suppose so."

"Your father is happy, too, isn't he?"

"You bet! Mom, too! A lot of the kids in Cantwell say I have the happiest home anywhere."

"Well, perhaps your father meant that the key
to personal happiness is making others happy
through your work or your attitude or both.
You've made Mrs. Murdock very happy this summer. You're certainly making a lot of the town
youngsters happy. And you yourself appear to be
happier than you were when you came down in
the middle of June."

Evalin mulled that over. She decided that she
really was happier now than she had been then.
Back in June, actually, she had felt both angry
and bitter because her folks had put her on probation. She had wondered how she would ever
get through a long summer of no dates and no
mad times with her friends in Princess Town. Yet
here it was August and the probation did not matter at all. There were so many things to do, actually, it was difficult to crowd them all into her
daily schedule. And all of them were really fun!
How could you hate working on the *Sea Hawk?*
You met so many interesting people each day and
saw so many interesting and beautiful things. And

how could she hate helping Jamie and Phil? Jamie could be so merry, and Phil could show her more secrets of Nature in three hours than she herself had been able to discover in years! And how could she hate being involved in the project?

Actually, Evalin decided, she would be one hundred percent happy if Grammy were well. Grammy's health was the only fly in the ointment, by golly!

Mr. Pike said abruptly: "You'll have to slow down a bit, Evalin. Jamie's a grand girl, but she's so anxious to please Mrs. Murdock that she's unable to be as strict with her as you. Mrs. Murdock has been walking again."

"No!"

"I'm afraid so. Now listen here: the main reason you took that job was to keep Mrs. Murdock's ferryboat running at no cost to Mrs. Murdock's health. That's still the main job. Very well. Now we come to all those telephone calls you received today. You can hardly interview all those people and inspect work and all that and still do your work on the ferryboat. So you need an assistant."

"Will I fry Jamie!"

"You will not! Jamie is at a disadvantage here. For the first time in many months she is getting proper food and clothing and earning money and having fun, too. Naturally, she's reluctant to do or say anything that might cause Mrs. Murdock to discharge her. No. There'd be no problem if you remembered your main responsibility and if you did the job you agreed to do."

Evalin could not meet his eyes, they looked so stern and disapproving.

"Why not ask Sue Winthrop to be your assistant?"

"The kids don't like her, Mr. Pike."

"It isn't necessary for them to like her, you know."

"The trouble is this, Mr. Pike. Say that Sue invites a boy to play miniature golf with her. Say that the boy refuses. She hates people who don't do what she wants them to do. Very well. Then say that a couple of days later Sue has to inspect that boy's work. Will she be fair, objective, or will she give that particular boy a bad time? Or suppose that Sue's disapproval of that particular boy's work is justified. Will the boy believe she isn't secretly trying to get back at him?"

Mr. Pike laughed softly. "That sounds pretty complicated to me."

"Well, it is complicated," Evalin insisted. "This is what I mean. The person who interviews potential employers and who inspects the work has an awful lot of power. And don't think for even a single second all the kids don't know that. Well, I've always gotten along pretty well with everybody. Rightly or wrongly, I'm trusted. Even if I do crazy fool things, the kids sort of understand that I'm doing my level best and they make allowances for my inexperience. Like the other afternoon when I scolded a boy for not raking up all that litter from around the rosebushes. He told me very, very tactfully that the so-called litter was really peat moss and that peat moss is used as a mulch around the rosebushes to keep the ground from drying out."

"It is," Mr. Pike said. "But see here, Mouse, I thought you and Sue patched up your differences.

I know she's helped you a few times recently."

Evalin nodded gloomily. There was the real trouble, she thought. Ever since that breakfast with Sue and their serious talk, Sue and she had been pretty friendly. Now that Sue understood no one could be first in everything, she was proving to be a darned sweet girl. Still, what right had she, Evalin Mitchell, to decide Sue could be trusted to assist her with the project? Suppose the decision turned out to be the worst one in history? A lot of the town kids could be hurt. The project could actually be ruined. And her first duty, it seemed to Evalin, was to the project.

"Afraid to take a chance?" Mr. Pike asked.

Evalin admitted she was.

"I'll tell you something interesting," Mr. Pike said. "You didn't apply for the work you're doing for the project. Mrs. Riley approached you because she thought you have good judgment. Well, you have to use your judgment. Using your judgment is really a part of the responsibility you've assumed. If you're inclined to give Sue a chance, then do so. But I'd certainly not hold back, if I were you, for fear your judgment is wrong. People who fear to make the wrong decisions end up making no decisions, and you do have to make decisions, it seems to me."

Grammy came out of Murdock House, *walking*. Evalin jumped up and went rushing to the house, so genuinely upset that Grammy looked embarrassed. Grammy said, "All right, Mouse, all right! I just become so tired of that blasted chair!"

"And you've been walking on the boat, too," Evalin charged hotly. "Grammy, that's unfair! You know very well that poor Jamie is too afraid of losing her job to make you stay in that wheel chair. Grammy, that's *mean*!"

Grammy glared at Mr. Pike as he came into the yard. Mr. Pike said sturdily: "Yup, I've told her. No sass, now, because I'm still taking over whether you like it or not, Mrs. Murdock."

"I'll never marry a tattletale!"

"What about marrying me in September, Mrs. Murdock, before the brown mouse goes back home?"

Grammy made a squeaking sound and sat down and looked very flustered. Evalin tactfully went into the house. And then and there she did what she had been longing to do ever since Sue Winthrop had helped her with Mr. Adams. She telephoned Sue and asked Sue to be her assistant. Sue's answer thrilled her. Sue told her, with a tremble in her voice: "Evalin, I feel honored."

Chapter 16

At the Strawberry Goo on Saturday, the reactions of the gang to Sue's appointment were mixed. Tom Crowell declared he would not trust Sue Winthrop as far as he could throw a bull elephant. Doris Craddock predicted that from that moment on Sue would make everyone dance to her tune. Ted Pillsbury, on the other hand, came to Evalin's table and shook her hand. "Clever," Ted said. "Whatever Sue does, she does enthusiastically. Sue can fight just as hard for you as against you. I think she'll do a darned good job."

Having Ted's support encouraged Evalin to believe she had made a correct decision. More and more, Evalin was beginning to think Ted

Pillsbury was the most level-headed boy she had ever known. What a different opinion from that she had had of him the day he had ordered her to fade from his life! It all tended to prove, Evalin thought, that a person was silly to decide impulsively that another person was hopeless. Thanks to Ted, the picketing of the *Sea Hawk* had ended. Thanks to Ted, the town kids' resentment of the summer kids was ending. Thanks to Ted, the opposition to Sue's appointment would end, too.

After the powwow, Evalin paid a visit to Mrs. Riley in the *Times* building. She found Mrs. Riley daydreaming and sipping coffee at her desk. Mrs. Riley blushed prettily after Evalin had coughed three times to attract her attention. Much to Evalin's amusement, Mrs. Riley then proceeded to act tough in exactly the same way Grammy always acted tough when Grammy was feeling embarrassed. "Mitchell," Mrs. Riley said, "I didn't appreciate receiving a column from Sue Winthrop this week. You're supposed to write the weekly project report."

"Sue asked if she might try it, ma'am."

"She doesn't write warmly enough. I will say that she appears to know more about punctuation than you, but her writing fails to stimulate me. Are you too busy to write the column?"

"I thought that if Sue had her name published in the paper every once in a while, she'd become more and more interested in the project."

"Vanity!"

"Well, they use the same technique at school, sometimes, to stimulate the students."

Mrs. Riley chuckled. "Watch out," she warned. "You may develop into a psychologist! Very well. If you think it wise, we'll publish Sue Winthrop's work from time to time. What's on your mind?"

"I wondered how the project is progressing. I've deliberately given everything to Sue to handle."

"Well, the project is working out quite well, as a matter of fact. About fifty youngsters have found money-making opportunities so far. Almost as important, more and more men and women are showing an interest in supporting the project.

I'm particularly pleased about that. There are so many chores a youngster can perform for adults if the adults will just give him a chance. By the way, who hatched the idea of checking up on the quality of the work the youngsters perform?"

"Sue."

"Really?"

Evalin chuckled. "Frankly, I didn't welcome the idea at first. I thought the kids would resent the inspections. But they don't. I guess they realize that if the work is really done properly, they'll make friends and get other work."

Mrs. Riley sat thinking a couple of minutes. Outside, all the world darkened as the sun was engulfed by a great gray cloud. Studying the cloud, Evalin wondered if there would be rain. It was a queer sort of day, Evalin thought. Never had she known the Eastern Shore to be so humid. She rather hoped it would rain. She hated sticky weather.

Mrs. Riley shrugged. "It's all up to you," she said. "If you think you need an assistant and if Sue continues to do good work, I won't interfere with whatever arrangements you two make. But as I've said, I prefer your columns, and I hope you'll write your fair share of them."

Dan Wyatt came along in an old Chevrolet and parked at the curb and beeped once. Mrs. Riley gave him an appraising glance and smiled rather girlishly and wistfully. "Ah," she said, "to be young again and a part of the crowd. I'm quite happy, by the way, that you two have patched up your differences."

"As a matter of fact," Evalin confessed, blushing, "so am I, ma'am."

With Dan, Evalin went on to the last of the calls she wanted to make that morning. But Sue was out on project business, a fact that seemed to delight Mr. Winthrop hugely. "Just between us," he told Evalin, "I hardly know my girl these days. She stays awake nights dreaming up ways to get work for this one or that. The funny thing is, Sue never much cared about work before. I remember times when she actually called a servant into the living room to get a book from the bookcase for her. What have you done to her, eh?"

"Oh, Sue just needed something to do, sir. Ask any teacher you want. The chances are, she'll tell you that girls Sue's age must have something to do, something that really matters."

"Well, I'm darned glad, Evalin, that you took her into the project. I was beginning to wonder if Sue would ever settle down and get her teeth into something important. Now look; I've been doing some thinking about this project. The more I think about it, the more I like it. Kids have to be educated. Those who are mentally qualified have to go on to college. Now college costs money, as we all know, and money can be a problem, as we all know, too. Well, I've been thinking of establishing a vegetable cannery on the Eastern Shore, and it may as well be established in Princess Town. There'd be good summer jobs for about sixty youngsters. Think they'd be interested?"

Evalin was so thrilled she could have kissed him. Interested? The kids would *leap* at the chance to work in that cannery! And just think what a big difference the availability of good summer jobs would make in the lives of Sandra and Doris and Mike and Tom and all her other friends in Princess Town! If they saved most of their wages, college would be a probability rather than just a remote possibility. And if the kids completed their education—wow!

"I think they'd be interested," Evalin said laughingly. "Glory smoke!"

"Are you?"

"I?"

Mr. Winthrop sat down and looked around the big living room and lighted a cigar. "You," he then said. "Now listen to me a moment. Your folks have a good income, and I know you're under no pressure to work. But work is as good for you, young lady, as it is for my Sue. You were wild and woolly this last year. I know about that, because your father and I discussed you two or three times. Well, see what work and responsibility have done for you this summer. Having something serious to think about has gotten a lot of silly notions out of your head. All right. The truth is that I decided three months ago to locate a plant here. That's why I've spent so much of the summer down here. I never thought about hiring youngsters, frankly, but the more I think about it now, the better I like it. So who's to help me hire the youngsters and keep an eye on them? I'd like to hire you, from the middle of June until the middle of September. Interested?"

Evalin gulped.

"Business administration is a good career," Mr. Winthrop said. "You have a talent for handling people, I've noticed, so I imagine you'd do especially well in personnel management. Now don't make any decision now. I'll discuss the matter with you up north this winter. But think about it, eh?"

When Evalin went back to the car, her thoughts were spinning crazily. Dan Wyatt, noticing her expression, asked if she had had another scrap with Sue. Evalin told him about Mr. Winthrop's plans, and Dan whistled and then said quickly: "I'm applying right now, boss lady. If I could be sure of three summers of work, I could go to college, all right."

"To study what?"

"Dentistry."

"Ugh!"

Dan laughed. "If you had a toothache you'd be darned glad there are dentists in the world."

Evalin settled down on the seat as Dan headed back to Murdock House. "Actually," she told him, "I haven't decided to take the job. Dan, a year's a long, long time. I have a whole junior year at high school to complete! How do I even know that next year I'll come down to the Eastern Shore? Mom and Dad have talked about taking me to Thailand next year."

"But this is your place! That's your job! Look, you can't hang onto your parents forever, you know. You have to make your own place in the world."

And this lovely town of Princess Town, Evalin thought, would certainly be a nice place to be.

The sky was quite dark when they reached Murdock House. Dan said knowingly, "There'll be a storm, all right. Want extra help on the boat, just in case?"

Grinning, Evalin pointed to Jamie and Phil aboard the *Sea Hawk*. "With three sailors to help her," Evalin bragged, "Grammy could run that boat through a hurricane. Thanks for the lift, Dan. I did promise Mr. Pike I'd make the last trip of the morning."

"Pleasure's all mine."

Evalin nipped into the house and changed into her working clothes. Every once in a while, as she dressed, she heard wind along the eaves. The sound excited her. The feeling of storm in the air stimulated her. She loped to the *Sea Hawk* and looked at the dark sky and green-gray water and whitecaps and grinned contentedly at Grammy. "I always did want to sail in a storm," she told Grammy. "Can we take a chance?"

"A good captain never takes chances, Mouse. That won't be a storm; just a little blow with some rain. You get those lazy swabs moving!"

Evalin swaggered forward and told the lazy "swabs" to get moving. Phil said it would be a mean storm, and he told Grammy they ought to stay at the pier. But when Grammy told him she'd not have a mutiny, thank you, Phil went to the stern line and waved Jamie up forward. Grammy tooted the whistle, and they were off!

The fat *Sea Hawk* pushed forward powerfully, swaying a bit on the rough water but never losing headway and never yawing. Up forward, Jamie laughed at her brother. "Gloomy Gus!" Jamie teased. "You expect a cloud to come down and bite you?"

Thunder roared overhead. About three seconds later, a great streak of lightning shot across the sky, and thunder roared again. Suddenly all the water around them turned glass smooth and dark green. Phil yelled, "Mrs. Murdock, it's gonna hit, it's gonna hit!" His voice frightened Evalin. Evalin loped back to Grammy. Grammy looked at her in the strangest way, her face purple-red and puffy, her eyes bulging. Grammy said, "Mouse, take the wheel, please. Don't drift, Mouse, you understand?"

Again thunder boomed, and as if that had been the signal the elements had been awaiting, the storm broke. A great wind came swishing down the river, kicking up the water, driving great sheets of rain into Evalin's face. The rain came down so hard it seemed to blot out the world, and the river became so rough the old *Sea Hawk* actually began to pitch and toss. Evalin screeched for Grammy to take over, but Grammy never moved. Slumped in her wheel chair, her head hanging, Grammy sat in the wheel chair like a person dead.

Jamie came fighting through the rain and wind to the controls behind the windscreen. Jamie looked at Grammy and gave a peculiar cry that brought Phil on the run. Phil and Jamie rolled Grammy away to the galley, and then Phil came back and yelled: "Starboard, starboard, starboard!"

Evalin swung the wheel frantically, understanding that Phil wanted her to point the *Sea Hawk* into the sudden, savage storm. Phil reached out and revved up the motor. "Ride 'er out!" Phil ordered. "Don't try to land; ride 'er out!"

Impulsively, Evalin tried to give Phil the wheel. But Phil rushed back to the galley, leaving her alone in the storm world to combat the elements as best she could.

Soon all the sky seemed to be aflame with almost continuous flashes of lightning. Soon the constant roars of thunder left Evalin with a great roaring inside her head. Suddenly the glass part of the windscreen was blown away. Now the wind tore at Evalin as if determined to blow her away, too. She had to crouch to get protection from the wooden part of the windscreen, and of course the *Sea Hawk* yawed and had to be forced back to point dead into the storm.

And on and on went the storm, lashing itself into a fury, kicking up actual waves on the river, battering the *Sea Hawk,* sluicing it down with tons of rain. Evalin grew tired at the wheel. A knife-like pain shot across her back and down her legs. Once a crazy toss of the *Sea Hawk* sent her sprawling. She almost remained on the wet cold deck, so tired and aching she wanted to close her eyes and sleep. Somehow, though, she pulled herself to her feet and went, dripping wet and bruised, back to the wheel. A wave crashed over the low stern deck, then another and another. Suddenly it occurred to Evalin that if she did not swing the bows around those waves might sink them all. Straining, gasping, she worked the wheel and forced the *Sea Hawk* into the storm once more. But now, knowing she could not hang on too many minutes longer, she pulled the whistle cord and sounded the distress signal for all the world to hear.

Where was Grammy?

Why were Jamie and Phil staying in the galley with Grammy?

What in the world had the storm done to Grammy?

A dreadful thought flashed across Evalin's mind. Grammy was dead! Grammy had died of a heart attack in the storm!

A great sob came from Evalin's throat, but she never released the wheel, never abandoned the *Sea Hawk* to the raging storm. She was still at the wheel, an exhausted, pathetic slip of a girl, when the storm petered out and fishermen from Carter Hollow and Princess Town could answer her distress signals at last. . . .

Chapter 17

The next week was the longest, scariest week Evalin had ever experienced. Dr. McGrath told her sternly to keep away from the hospital in Birch Corners, but it was all Evalin could do to obey his orders. She knew now that her grandmother had indeed suffered a stroke aboard the *Sea Hawk* and that her grandmother's condition was critical. Mr. Pike told her these things, and more. The day after the storm, while Evalin was moping on the porch, Mr. Pike told her: "The *Sea Hawk* has made her last trip. Mrs. Murdock won't ever take her out again, I'll tell you that. What she'll need from now on is a tamer life on shore."

Evalin looked at the ferryboat. Phil and Jamie were working aboard her, checking on the damage that had been done and cleaning up. In a peculiar way, it bothered Evalin to think in terms of the *Sea Hawk* being beached forever. The *Sea Hawk* had not let them down. Although she had certainly not been built to endure the punishment of practically a hurricane, the *Sea Hawk* had withstood the savagery of the storm as well as any other craft could have done.

"Great kids, those," Mr. Pike said, pointing to Jamie and Phil Holloway. "They saved your lives, you know. First, Phil saved your lives by pointing the *Sea Hawk* into the storm and ordering you to ride the storm out. Had you done anything else, you'd have been killed. And Jamie saved your grandmother's life by getting her into the galley and stretched out on the floor. Great kids, those. I'm darned glad you made it your business to help them."

So was Evalin.

And she continued to be glad throughout the long and scary week she sat waiting for her folks to come from Thailand. It was as if Jamie and Phil were members of her personal family now. Of all people, Jamie took over in Murdock House. Jamie did the cooking and Jamie prevented her from moping. And outdoors, Phil took over. One day, because Phil insisted, Evalin went with him to the marshland beyond the cannery to see the birds. Another day, again because Phil insisted, they took the catboat into Pirate's Cove Creek and explored the creek thoroughly. And who arranged for a Saturday afternoon cookout for all of Evalin's crowd in Princess Town? Phil and Jamie. Not a word about it, either. Sue Winthrop came along while Evalin was lying in the hammock Jamie had strung between two sycamore trees. "Lazy pig!" Sue teased. "What a lovely outfit, too! Won't you be the sensation, the beloved darling, in those dear grubby denims!"

"Hi," Evalin said, sitting up. "How's the project coming along?"

"Fine. I've even lined up a job for myself next summer. Administrative assistant to you in Daddy's new plant. We'll have a ball!"

"I never accepted that job!"

"But you will," Sue predicted. "How can you let everybody down? Did I let you down once you made me your assistant? Did Jamie and Phil let you down? Did any of the town kids let you down after you helped them to find jobs? You bet not! And I'll tell you why. Because a lot of people who say they care about people really don't. But you do. Deep down inside, you actually do! You never once scolded anyone who put you in the deep freeze or picketed the pier. You could have told Mrs. Riley to find someone else to help with the project. And you certainly didn't have to help the Holloway kids after Phil was so rude to you. But you did. And take my own case. I was scared to death the morning Daddy insisted I invite you to breakfast. I was wondering how I'd wiggle out of things after you had told Daddy how mean I'd been. But you never even told him. Instead, you made me your assistant. Well, what does all that add up to? Just this, Miss Evalin Mitchell. Because you care about them, the kids care about themselves, and you, too. Because you care about me, I care about you and I have respect for myself now, too. Darn it, all my life I've been hungry to be liked for myself, not for Daddy's money. And I'm being liked now, honestly!"

"Just the same—"

"We're better people, all of us, Evalin, because of you. All right. So you can't make us worse people again by proving all along you never did care for us deep down inside. And you'd prove that if you refused the job Daddy has offered you. Why? Because Daddy won't hire kids unless you agree to be the wheel."

"That's crazy!"

"Don't you call my Daddy crazy!"

Sandra came along, then Doris. In a few minutes there we е about forty kids in the yard, each carrying something for a cookout, each going out of his way to assure Evalin everything would turn out just fine.

What interested Evalin most about the cookout was the friendly attitude each kid had toward Jamie and Phil. Some squealing girls put a chef's hat on Phil and appointed him Lord High Muck-a-Muck of the Feast. The boys cornered Jamie, and someone got a portable record player going, and Jamie was Queen of a Ball at which, by golly, she was the only girl present. And very nice things were done for Jamie and Phil, too, in other ways. After chow, while everyone was sitting around digesting the hamburgers and a million other things as well, Sandra climbed to her feet and got a big parcel from Dan Wyatt's car and made a speech.

"Tykes," Sandra said, "lend me your ears. Jamie, you come up here and take this present. And why do we give you a present? Elementary, my dear Watson! Because it just so happened you helped to save the lives of two females all of us happen to love. Open up and weep!"

Three lovely dresses for Jamie!

A beautiful dull green suit for Jamie!

Shoes and stockings and lingerie for Jamie!

All her size, too!

"By golly," Sandra said to the weeping Jamie, "we must love you a whole lot, because each of us chipped in from our hard-earned money, and we badgered a lot of adults to chip in, too. Love and kisses from all of us."

And for Phil?

Grinning broadly, Ted Pillsbury actually drove a jalopy into the yard. "Old son," Ted said, "we bummed this heap from the used-car dealer in Birch Corners, and about a hundred of us guys really jazzed her up. I won't say love and kisses, but any time you want a nose punched, you ask us to do it for you. Okay?"

They were her people, Evalin thought, profoundly stirred. They were her friends. All her life they would be her people and her friends. No matter where she went or what she did in the years ahead, she would remember each of them always. If they took, they gave. If they could be difficult, they could also be sweet. If they were capable of putting you into a deep freeze, they were also capable of making you feel among the most deeply loved and wanted persons on earth.

The cookout and all the sentimental goo seemed to help. That evening, for the first time since the storm, Evalin had no trouble falling asleep, and she slept soundly. The next morning, when her parents came home browned and tired from Thailand, she was herself again. Perhaps because she was, the get-reacquainted chatter amused her.

"Duck," her mother said, "you've sprouted. Glory be, you're up to my shoulders."

"It happens," Dr. Mitchell said with mock gloominess. "They're cute only for such a little while. Soon the hair turns gray and the wrinkles form. Nice to have known you, Mouse."

Evalin's father hurried off to Birch Corners, of course, in Phil's jalopy. Evalin showed her mother to the bedroom next to Grammy's, and she and Jamie lugged the two suitcases upstairs. Jamie brought up hot tea and some sandwiches and then gave Evalin a cheery wink and scooted off.

"I always did crave red hair like hers," Mrs. Mitchell said. "Did I ever tell you that when I was your age I actually dyed my hair red?"

"No!"

Mrs. Mitchell chuckled. "You'll discover as you go along that adults were once young, too.

But may I also say that when I was your age I lacked your character? I think I do want to say that, dear. It's been a rugged summer, hasn't it?"

"Not really."

Something about her mother seemed strange to Evalin. She finally identified that strangeness as *smallness.* Her mother seemed so much smaller than she had been back at the middle of June. Yet here it was only September, and in just twelve or thirteen weeks no one could possibly shrink that much even in a hot country that dehydrated you!

"Have I developed a third eye or something?" Mrs. Mitchel asked. She smiled that crooked little smile Evalin had always considered so cute. "You're looking at me as if you didn't recognize me."

"You seem smaller, Mother Duck."

"Naturally. And I'll seem smaller and smaller to you as time goes on, I fear. That's been going on all your life, of course. Growth, growth, growth! A fine thing, all in all. I wonder, however, if your intellect has grown any since

February, say."

Evalin grinned and sat down companionably beside her. "You won't believe this, I know," she said, "but I've been taking lessons on how to study from Sue Winthrop, of all people. Where did I find the time? Who knows? Zounds, but I've been busy!"

"Any fun?"

Evalin looked inward at her memories of the so-called vacation on the Eastern Shore. There had been much fun, she discovered, even if it had not been the sort of fun she had anticipated before she had gotten on the train in Massachusetts. Certainly the ferryboat trips had been fun. Certainly her expeditions with Phil and Jamie had been fun. And certainly it had been fun to work on the project.

"Loads of fun," she told her mother. "It seems peculiar, though, in a way. Basically, I abhor responsibility and schedules and things like that."

"You'll learn to love them in the end, dear. That, too, is part of growing up. Now hear the decisions we made aboard the plane. For your information only, Mr. Pike and your grandmother will marry. You will come home with us, of course. Jamie and Phil Holloway will live here with Mr. and Mrs. Pike, and I suspect that Mr. Pike and Phil will keep the *Sea Hawk* afloat. Next summer? Well, that's up to you. You may come to Thailand with us, or you may work here for Mr. Winthrop. Oh, he cleared his offer with us before he made it to you, naturally. Parents stick together in matters such as that, believe me."

Evalin said quickly: "Here, Mom. Actually, you don't need me in Thailand."

"Well, we'll see. One more matter. Your grandmother will not die, if that's been worrying you. She will have to be careful the rest of her life, meaning no more sailing, no more heavy physical activity. It's too bad, but that's how life is."

"If Mr. Pike and Phil could keep the boat going, Mom, then Phil would have a nice job waiting for him when he finishes school. That would be wonderful, wouldn't it?"

Mrs. Mitchell smiled and rose and went to her

suitcase and opened it and drew out a small lacquered box. She said: "Catch!" Evalin caught. Evalin tried to open the box, all excited, but the box was locked. Her mother laughed and said: "In Chiengmai a few weeks ago, an old man told me there is a key for everything, even for happiness. But it has to be earned, he said. Isn't that interesting?"

Evalin's heart began to drum. She could see in her mother's eyes that her probation was over.

"I demand the key!" Evalin said, laughing.

"Well, then, for Grammy and Jamie and Phil and Sue and all the other kids in town, here's the key. I would like to say, Evalin, that you have pleased me very much."

What was in the box?

The ruby earrings!

Evalin put them on. They hurt her ears, but who cared? My, but the junior boys at Cantwell High had a treat in store for them this year!

Then Evalin saw the gift card in the box, and the words written by her mother drove all the silliness from her mind. From Mom Duck to Lady

Duck, indeed!

Carefully, Evalin returned the earrings to the box. "It may take some doing," she said shakily, "but I'll try to wear them with honor, Mom."

Humming, deeply contented, Evalin went to Phil aboard the *Sea Hawk* and told him that the old girl would make many more trips to and from Princess Town on the broad and beautiful Princess River.

Phil's smile, surprisingly, pleased her more than the earrings had. Now why was that? Evalin wondered.

Zounds, the things a person had to learn!